"A fun, sassy read! A cross between Erma Bombeck and Candace Bushnell, reading Jenny Gardiner is like sinking your teeth into a chocolate cupcake…you just want more."
--**Meg Cabot**, NY Times bestselling author of *Princess Diaries*, *Queen of Babble* and more, on *Sleeping with Ward Cleaver*

"With a strong yet delightfully vulnerable voice, food critic Abbie Jennings embarks on a soulful journey where her love for banana cream pie and disdain for ill-fitting Spanx clash in hilarious and heartbreaking ways. As her body balloons and her personal life crumbles, Abbie must face the pain and secret fears she's held inside for far too long. I cheered for her the entire way."
--**Beth Hoffman**, NY Times bestselling author of *Saving CeeCee Honeycutt* on *Slim to None*

"Jenny Gardiner has done it again--this fun, fast-paced book is a great summer read."
--**Sarah Pekkanen**, NY Times bestselling author of *The Opposite of Me*, on *Slim to None*

"As Sweet as a song and sharp as a beak, ***Bite Me*** really soars as a memoir about family--children and husbands, feathers and fur--and our capacity to keep loving though life may occasionally bite."
--**Wade Rouse**, bestselling author of *At Least in the City Someone Would Hear Me Scream*

LOVE IS IN THE HEIR

by Jenny Gardiner
(book four of the Royals of Monaforte series)

Copyright © 2015 by Jenny Gardiner

ISBN-13: 978-1517157159
ISBN-10: 1517157153

All rights reserved, including the right to reproduce this book or portions thereof in any form whatsoever.

All characters in this book are fiction and figments of the author's imagination. This ebook is licensed for your personal enjoyment only. This ebook may not be re-sold or given away to other people. If you would like to share this book with another person, please purchase an additional copy for each person you share it with. Thank you for respecting the author's work.
http://jennygardiner.net/

Chapter One

PIPPA Grimaldi, a decidedly modern Monafortian duchess and all-around life of the party, didn't normally ogle men. It just wasn't her style. And she'd certainly never held up any man in the royal family as anything but friend material. That is until she ran into His Royal Highness Prince Christopher, Duke of Esmeralda—Topher, for short—for the first time in many years.

Pippa and Topher, third in line to the throne of Monaforte, had a history together, and not such a great one. Back when she was fourteen, Pippa, best friends with Topher's brother Zander and a regular at the palace, had wandered in on Topher with his pants down, in mid, uh, self-service mode.

Mortified, Pippa had burst into nervous laughter, then hightailed it out of Topher's room to Zander's so fast that her friend immediately noticed something was wrong. And once Zander—long the bad boy prince in the family—latched on to what she'd encountered, he never let it go. Poor Topher was dubbed "the Wanker" by his older brother and teased mercilessly by his siblings for years.

Over the years, it had been obvious that Topher took great pains to avoid Pippa's presence, because aside from his continued embarrassment over the Episode, whenever the two of them were together, invariably the whole thing was dredged up yet again, much to his deep chagrin.

And so when Topher encountered Pippa at the reception following the royal wedding of his brother Adrian, he could only hope that royal decorum would trump his siblings' propensity for jocularity. The last thing he needed while suited up in his regal princely military garb for this shindig was to be reduced to that shamed teenager of years earlier, with a round of guffaws and elbows to the side while the siblings all referenced Topher's manual dexterity. Sometimes even his usually sweet sister, Isabella, got in on the act. And it would only make matters worse if his new sister-in-law, Emma, joined the fray.

He really just hoped that after he'd been gone for so long, maybe at last the event had been tucked away in the cobwebbed attic of family lore, finally forgotten, laid to merciful rest. It always amazed him that no matter how old you got or how accomplished you became, you were always brought to your knees by some stupid happening in your life you wished you'd never committed. Or at least wished you'd locked the door for.

Of course one thing he always, always, always held close to him about that day was this: the only reason he was in the midst of the deed at that particular moment was that Pippa had showed up at the palace in a particularly skimpy skirt and tight tee that highlighted her burgeoning assets. And what gangly, awkward teenage boy could resist that? As the two-years-younger brother, Topher had always had a little bit of a crush on his brother's friend, but he'd also had never confided that to a soul. And so in deference to her dignity, he realized all the more that that fact needed to remain tucked away in his mind only as it would merely serve to humiliate Pippa.

But from then on, he forever associated Pippa with his shame from that event, and rarely did he ever dare to entertain thoughts of Pippa as anything but a family friend.

Jenny Gardiner

Topher, his gentle gray eyes and wavy dark hair highlighted by the bright blue royal military uniform he wore, had just finished his drink at the wedding reception when his brother Zander pulled him into a conversation unwittingly.

"Plus," Zander said to his beautiful blond, blue-eyed girlfriend Andi, extending his arm as his younger brother came toward them. "Soon this strapping young man will find himself a woman and the paps will latch on to him instead. Even though I *am* the much-better-looking brother."

Andi had seemingly pulled off the impossible, taming the womanizing Zander, known for his scampish good looks with his scruffy dark hair, perpetual five-o'clock shadow, and mesmerizing green eyes.

Apparently Andi was fearful of the paparazzi, which had caused her to flee her blossoming romance with Zander, and Zander had only somehow lured her back to Monaforte just in time for the wedding.

Topher looked at him with wide eyes like he was crazy. "Yeah, right. Besides, don't hold your breath on that," he said. "The chances of my marrying anytime in the next millennium are slim to none."

"That's what I said, and look at me now," Adrian said as he walked up to the group. The oldest of the siblings, Adrian was devastatingly handsome, and on this, his wedding day, his brilliant sapphire eyes were alight with happiness. "Zander, looks like finally your invisible girlfriend here took pity on you?" He nodded toward Andi, who blushed.

Topher was thrilled the conversation was focusing on

Love Is in the Heir

Zander's romance, but only then did he notice that Pippa was lurking on the fringe of the conversation. Pippa—looking so damned hot in the halter gown Topher tried desperately not to stare at because it highlighted her breasts and her shapely waist—was the last thing he needed to think of right then. Those thoughts could get him into a lot of trouble. Her hazel eyes seemed to sparkle against the warm melon color of her flowing gown.

Two times two is four, four times four is sixteen, sixteen times sixteen is two hundred and fifty-six, he repeated in his head, tamping down all potentially damning sexual thoughts involving the woman, including the time he'd seen her naked when she came out of the shower of the palace pool house when she was seventeen. *Two times two is four, four times four is sixteen, sixteen times sixteen is two hundred and fifty-six.*

Topher could feel the front of his dress blues getting just a little bit snug, and he continued distracting himself with simple mathematical equations until he could extricate himself from the present company. He glanced out of the corner of his gray eyes to see that Pippa's cascading brown curls—which as a teenager had looked so sexy on her, tumbling over her shoulders like a riotous waterfall—had been pulled up in a loose chignon, her hair topped with the obligatory tiara that most women of royalty wore to such events. Hers was interlaced with tiny flowers, and soft strands of curls framed her face, which had grown only more beautiful with age. He thought she looked like quite the princess herself, even if she was actually a duchess. Not that there was anything wrong with that, but in the pecking order of royalty, she wasn't a princess. Even if she looked like the fairy tale version of one.

"Don't worry, Andi," Pippa said, piping into the

conversation. "We all take care of each other here. You won't be bombarded by anyone trying to get at you. Just a little here and there. Otherwise we cut 'em off at the knees." She jokingly made a slicing motion across the throat.

Topher knew only too well how everyone took care of each other around here, even when it involved totally dicking on your brothers. Slicing across the throat indeed. It might have been easier for him if they *had* just slit his throat. Lost in thought, he rejoined the conversation as Pippa continued talking.

"I must say, most intriguing of all is little Topher here," Pippa said, turning to him. "I don't think I've seen you since you were a scrawny kid. You're looking awfully filled out." She eyed him up and down with a look of hunger on her face.

"Down, girl," Zander said, tapping on Pippa's head. "I think Topher is allergic to women."

His brother discreetly flipped him the finger.

Awfully filled out?

If he didn't know better, he'd think he was perhaps a baby wildebeest and Pippa a very hungry leopard about to pounce.

Topher said a mental prayer that this was not the segue he'd been dreading and breathed a sigh of relief when, not a half a minute later, he was saved by the arrival of Adrian's new bride, Emma, ravishingly beautiful with her chestnut curls loosely pinned up and tucked behind a dazzling tiara. Her hazel eyes were wet with tears of happiness. *Thank goodness for all this wedding nonsense as a distraction.*

This time he was spared.

Love Is in the Heir

Pippa tried to concentrate on the conversation at hand. Something to do with Adrian and Emma's wedding and then something more about Emma's good friend Caroline and Adrian's best friend Darcy showing up to the wedding engaged, of all things. Which apparently had happened after Darcy's sister Clementine orchestrated a fabulous fake out at a party at Pippa's family estate, which had left Darcy thinking Zander was hitting on Caroline. At that very party, Zander then ended up hooking up with Andi, with whom Pippa had worked at a refugee camp in Africa months earlier.

Pippa couldn't help but wonder why everyone around her seemed to be finding soul mates while she only seemed to find another excuse to host a party or play cupid with her friends' relationships. Not that she was looking or anything; she was too busy to really worry about dealing with a boyfriend. But sometimes it seemed like it would be nice to have someone to maybe just go on a date with. Or make out with. Or more. She hadn't scratched that itch in as long as she could remember. The opportunity hadn't presented itself when Pippa was working overseas in various philanthropic capacities, which she did as manager of Zander's Prince's Trust foundation.

Her thoughts migrated to Topher, standing several feet from her—though she knew if he'd had his way, there'd be several hundred feet separating the two of them. It had always been that way. Well, not quite always. But certainly since the Episode. Honestly, Pippa could still close her eyes and conjure up the image of Topher in that compromising position. It had always left her feeling conflicted—embarrassed, no doubt, but kind of hot and bothered too.

She'd never seen such a thing before, and it was the first time she'd ever seen one of those things live and in action. God, she still felt like a rookie in the sex department. She'd had a handful of less-than-compelling relationships in college and since but nothing that aroused much, well, arousal. Most of the guys she'd dated were kind of boring, often trying to rub shoulders with royalty and rarely interested in Pippa as a person.

She tried to discreetly check out Topher from the corner of her eye. He looked so damned handsome garbed in full military regalia: the crisp blue uniform, the sheathed sword, the sash, and all the medals. For the first time in forever, she felt her heart almost skip a beat over a guy. But could it be a worse guy? Thanks to Pippa, Topher was pegged with that embarrassing nickname by his brothers and couldn't get past something that undoubtedly the whole lot of them did daily under that palace roof. Poor Topher had had the grave misfortune of being caught red-handed. Literally.

She burst out laughing at her own mental joke, so loudly that everyone in the conversation turned to look at her. She tried to cover up her laughter by pretending to be choking on a sip of champagne. But her eyes met Topher's, and in that brief exchange, they both knew they were each revisiting that moment yet again.

Pippa felt horrible; the poor guy could never live down such an isolated instance of being caught in the act. No thanks to her.

Chapter Two

TOPHER spent dinner engaged in conversation with some princess from Sweden or Denmark or another very blond country. She was absolutely stunning: deep blue eyes, natural blond hair (he assumed), perfect skin, knockout figure. Who could complain? In the days of his ancestors, no doubt he'd have been seated by the woman someone else had deigned it necessary for him to marry to forge a union with another country. Which made him quite happy this was not the culture nowadays. Because while this blond princess was incredibly hot, she was a bit boring. And her breath smelled. Besides, the last thing he wanted was a) to get married, and b) to be told he had to get married.

He was perfectly happy pursuing an advanced degree in marine biology and traveling to tropical climates to further his education. What he didn't need was an anchor in the form of a woman to tie him down. Nope, the type of anchor he preferred got lowered by a chain into sand at the bottom of the ocean when whatever boat he was sailing in was stopping for the night.

Nothing thrilled him more than being on the water, maybe kicking back with a steak fired up on the tiny grill on the back of the boat, a cold beer in his hand, and Bob Marley blasting on the speakers as the horizon swallowed the last of the day's sun in a spectacular show of color.

It's not that he didn't get into the whole dog-and-pony show of royalty. It's just that as third in line to the crown, he didn't have to bow to it quite so often, and he really did enjoy his freedom.

After dinner, the orchestra resumed playing, and he made a point to avoid his dinner companion before having to take things to the dance floor with her halitosis. But soon everyone was coupled up, and while he stood discreetly to the side, trying to not be seen and making small talk with people he really couldn't have cared less to talk to, he noticed Pippa stood not far away, perhaps also avoiding being seen. But she had a little bit of a sad look in her eyes, and it made his heart ache just a touch. Enough so he decided to approach her.

"You're looking somber for such a happy occasion," he said, handing her a flute of champagne he'd grabbed from a passing waiter.

Pippa shook her head. "Really?" she said. "I didn't mean to look so disconnected. I guess I'm just lost in thought."

Topher shook his head. "Please, don't tell me it's *that* thought." He decided it was high time to just make light of the damned thing, at least face-to-face with her.

She blushed and stammered her reply. "Oh, God, no! I mean, what thought?"

He lowered his head and arched his brow. "I think it goes without saying which thought."

"You mean *that*? Heavens no! I thought about that hours ago." She covered her mouth with her hands. "I mean no! I haven't been thinking about that! I haven't thought about that in ages. Actually, I've never thought about that." Pippa placed her hand over her eyes, mortified at her stupid remarks.

Topher repeated his dubious look. "I'm pretty sure if I thought about it when we first ran into each other, then you did."

Pippa cringed. "Oh Toph. It was so long ago. I'm really sorry. I didn't mean to resurrect that dead issue."

He laughed. "Not to worry. It never died, so you can't be accused of bringing it back to life. Like it or not, it's part of me now."

Pippa snorted. "Were it not for me, it wouldn't have remained in you long enough to be an issue."

She burst out laughing.

Topher smiled. "Yep, talk about wank-us interruptus." They both laughed. "I think it's time we let bygones be bygones with this one. What do you say?"

She nodded and looked down, blushing, which surprised Topher because he'd never known her to be one to wither at the first sign of awkward conversation. Of course, if any topic would make her cringe, this one certainly would be it.

"Yeah, sure."

Topher reached out his hand in invitation. "Would you like to dance?"

She smiled and nodded, and he pulled Pippa toward him to escort her to the dance floor as they joined the hundreds of guests around them. For several minutes, they just enjoyed each other's company, not saying a word.

When the orchestra started playing "Beyond the Sea," Topher pulled her closer, his hand around hers, pressed to his chest.

"This is my song," he said to her.

"You have your own anthem?"

Topher smiled. "Smart-ass," he said, tapping her on the nose with the tip of his finger. "No. But it reminds me of what makes me happiest: being out on the ocean."

Pippa cocked her head. "Oh really? You're a seagoing creature, are you?"

He nodded. "Something about the water calls to me. I've been pursuing my studies in marine biology, which takes me there often. I feel most at home when I'm bobbing on a boat in azure waters."

She nodded. "I understand what you're saying. It's like how I feel when I'm helping others. It's almost like I'm home too in a way."

"Helping others?"

"I work for Zander's charity," she said. "I often travel all over the world, whether I'm trying to enlist financial support or simply helping out with a project myself."

Topher had no idea that's what Pippa did. He was relieved she wasn't one of those trustafarian royals who rested on her daddy's bank account and shopped till she dropped. Though to be fair, he could easily be of the same ilk. Except that his parents would kill him if he tried that.

He found himself leaning in and whispering into her ear, "Wow, you're quite the international woman of mystery now."

Pippa shook her head. "Not so much. Just doing my job is all. But I'd love to hear about your travels."

Topher's eyes lit up. "I've been doing research on global warming and its impact on coral reefs. Which means I get to sail in beautiful locations all in the name of work."

"Not too shabby," she said. "I could almost be jealous about that."

"Maybe you could figure out a way to incorporate your charitable work with it and come sailing with me some time." Topher lifted his brow.

Pippa caught her breath. "Me? Sailing with you?"

Love Is in the Heir

Topher leaned back to take in her demeanor. "If it's something you might enjoy."

"Who doesn't love to sail?" she said. "But I've only sailed in the Mediterranean. What's it like in the Caribbean?"

He took a breath as he thought about it. "The water is so clear and comes in so many intoxicating shades of blue and green."

She smiled dreamily. "I never thought of those colors as intoxicating."

"Oh, but they are," he said. "Imagine looking at water the color of the finest turquoise stones. So pure and so inviting. It warms the soul."

"But what about sharks?"

Topher shook his head. "The biggest sharks you have to worry about there are of the human variety," he said. "Some of those beach bars, you just never know what type of disreputable men you'll encounter."

They both laughed.

"Disreputable, eh?" she said, cocking her eyebrow. "But surely you'd protect me from these shark men, right?"

Topher pulled her in tighter, thinking of how he'd always fantasized about being the man to take care of Pippa.

"That goes without saying," he said, his voice warm and rumbly in her ear.

"So what do you do with yourself when you're all the way out there in the ocean? How do you while away those long, lonely nights?"

He laughed. "To be honest, I've never had to concern myself with whiling away the hours. After a long day of work, the best I can muster is kicking back with a rum drink, grilling a steak, and blasting some music while absorbing yet another perfect sunset."

"By yourself?"

"There's always the skipper," he said.

"Now that's not exactly romantic," Pippa said. "You, a romantic sunset, and the captain."

Topher cracked up. "Unless the skipper's a woman," he said with a wink. "But seriously, you've got a point. Though I suppose some might find it romantic to be with the captain."

"What about companionship?" she asked. "Don't you find it lonely being out to sea so long?"

To be truthful, he occasionally did. It wasn't like you could pick up a one-night stand so easily when you were out to sea. Nor did you want to pick up someone you'd regret being stuck with. He tended to keep his philandering shoreside. Not that he philandered much, but still.

"You ask funny questions, you know that?" he said. "For someone who would barely talk to me for all those years, now you're concerned about my love life?"

Pippa paused as if to think for a minute, then broke into a wide grin. She glanced up into his face, and he knew exactly what triggered her reaction.

"Oh, my God," he said. "Surely you're not asking me that?"

She shook her head. "I wasn't at first," she said. "But then I started to think about it. I mean what else does one do when one is away from members of the opposite sex and the need is there?"

Topher grinned. "That might depend upon whom you're talking about. I am a man, after all," he said. "Let's leave it at that."

Love Is in the Heir

Pippa's mind flashed to the Episode, where the boy Topher was deeply engrossed in that very activity. Her face flushed as she recalled it.

"But," he added, "if you really want to discuss this, then what about you? What would you do all alone on a boat?"

She pursed her lips and thought about it. "Depends if the boat has thin walls."

He laughed some more. "I'm starting to think I'd love to be your skipper. I'd tell you the walls were fortified if that's what it took."

Pippa fake slapped him. "Why, how dare you, Prince Christopher!"

"Oh, so we're going to do it on a dare then?" he asked, pulling her in closer, whispering into her ear.

Her breathing got heavier as she thought about him all alone on a boat. "I could be persuaded," she whispered back into his ear.

It was Topher's turn for heavy breathing as he pressed himself up against her, leaving no question about where this discussion was going in his mind. "It's gotten so crowded in here. Perhaps we should continue this discussion somewhere a little more… private."

Pippa locked her hazel eyes on to his soulful gray ones. "But everyone would know we'd disappeared together."

He shook his head. "We'll slip off discreetly. You go first, and I'll follow in a minute. I think you know the way to my apartment."

She took a deep breath. "Our secret?"

He nodded. "No one will be the wiser."

Chapter Three

PIPPA'S heart was racing in her chest as she wandered the familiar-yet-now-silent hallways of the family corridor in the palace. What was she thinking? For that matter, what was *he* thinking? She had been persona non grata in Topher's world forever. And now all of a sudden he's wanting to slip off for, for, for what?

"Oh, God, what am I doing?" she muttered aloud, staring at the many portraits of Topher's ancestors gazing down at her. This is Topher! This is me! This is weird!

Yet she continued to walk quickly, managing to dodge a security guard who was pacing one hallway down from her. She slipped past the room that used to be Topher's back before each of his siblings got their own separate apartments, a nod to their adulthood. And it made her curious to imagine the difference between Topher then and Topher now. Like she'd said earlier, the man had filled out. Probably everywhere.

She paused and leaned against a doorway, catching her breath.

It's okay, Pips, she told herself. Nothing has to happen here. You can just go in there and act casual. You've known Topher since you were both children. He probably isn't even going there in his head. He likely just wants to show you pictures from his travels.

She heard impatient footsteps on the expensive Turkish rugs that spanned the corridor and looked up to see Topher racing toward her. He grabbed her hand and pulled her.

"Anyone see you?" he asked.

Pippa shook her head. "Thank God. I dodged a guard nearby, but that's it. Everyone was busy with the cake cutting when I slipped out."

They turned a corner and Topher punched in the security code to his apartment, opened the door, tugged her inside, and then pressed her up against the nearest wall.

Pippa wasn't sure if she was out of breath from running or from heightened anxiety about what she was about to do. Or not do. But it was too late to change her mind as Topher pulled her toward him, his hands traveling up and down along her sides as his face neared hers.

"I have no idea what I'm doing here," he said, his eyes locking on hers.

"That makes two of us," she said. "Are you sure this is a good idea?"

Far be it from her to be the voice of reason, but someone had to be.

"It's the best idea I've had in a long time," he said as his lips met hers and he pulled her in close.

Their hands grappled for skin, his roaming her exposed back, over her shoulders, and back again. Hers grasping beneath his uniform coat, working his shirt out from where it was tucked into his pants. Finally she found some skin, and her hands grazed over his lower back as their mouths clashed, both breathing hard and letting out the occasional moan of pleasure.

Topher reached for the zipper on the back of her dress only to find no such escape device. Pippa guided his hand around to show him it was on the side, and he deftly took it from there, stripping the zipper down and tugging the dress off in record time as his mouth meandered toward her neck, his tongue winding a trail toward her breasts.

She stood before him in nothing but a tiny blue thong, feeling extremely underdressed in his company.

"Hey," she said in a whisper. "This feels a little uneven here." She pointed at him and then at her.

He paused and then took his fill of her as she stood before him nearly naked. His breath hitched.

"We can fix that," he said, quickly unfastening the gold buttons of his jacket and flinging it to the side, then pulling off his shirt without undoing most of the buttons. Next went his sword, and he made fast work of his shoes and dress pants as well.

Pippa looked him up and down, his black boxer briefs unable to contain his excitement. "Now we're talking," she said with an impish smile.

They stood facing each other, her hands roaming over his chest as she kneaded them through the dark hair there while his made fast work over her breasts until he impatiently pulled her closer, settling his mouth over a nipple while Pippa moaned loudly, then made a face when she realized she was making noise which might draw attention to them. Until she realized no one was in this section of the palace, so who cared, and instead let out a louder moan still.

Pippa stood idly by as Topher continued to suck at her breast, which kept her busy enough, what with her hormone levels skyrocketing. But she felt the need to do something, so she wrapped a leg around Topher's legs until she lost her balance, pulling him down with her as she fell.

They both laughed as they landed on the soft Oriental rug, and then he spread her out and beheld her like a prized trophy he had to figure out where to place prominently.

"If you only knew how long I've wanted to do this," he said, leaning over her and placing a soft kiss on her lips.

She knit her eyebrows. "You're kidding, right?"

He shook his head. "I've nursed a crush on you I think since forever," he said. "A forbidden crush that I never thought I'd be able to act on."

She shook her head as if to clear the cobwebs. "On me? Like as in Pippa?"

He smiled. "Yes. As in Pippa."

"But I was the root cause of your life's torment."

"As well as the person I was thinking about when you walked in on me that day."

She gasped. "You're kidding?"

"Pips, don't you know how much I mooned over you when I was a kid? I hung on to your every word. I always wanted to be with you and Zander whenever you came over. And then when you started to grow up…"

"When you were doing *that*, you were thinking of this?" she said, pointing at herself.

"Do you have any idea what you wore that day?" he asked.

"Uh, no."

"For starters, one of those clingy, stretchy skirts that barely covered your ass," he said, remembering every inch of that meager thing. "And the shirt was some nearly nonexistent thing that hugged your breasts and bared your belly, and I could see the outline of your nipples, and honestly, Pips, I was a horny teenager. What the hell was I gonna do?"

She burst out laughing. "Oh, God. Had I known the trouble I'd get you in, I'd have worn a nun's frock. I'm sorry about that. I guess I didn't realize that anyone was paying attention to me or my body."

"Paying attention? Are you kidding? I was trying to devise a million and one ways to get those things off of you, all of which were running through my mind at precisely the moment you barged in on me."

She pouted. "I guess I should make up for the trouble I caused you."

"I wouldn't object, Your Honor."

She playfully pushed him onto his back and climbed atop, straddling his waist. "How's this for starters?" she said as she leaned over and stroked her tongue against his lips.

Topher opened up to her readily, and their tongues tangled as she wiggled her way down his body until her center was pressed up against his hard-on.

"I'd say that's a perfect place to start," he said in a whisper.

"So maybe if I end here…," she said as she maneuvered herself farther down, her tongue soon stroking his cock, which elicited a loud moan from Topher.

"Please, God, don't make that be the end," he said, reaching down for her. "But if you keep that up, this will all end too soon."

Pippa scooted her way back up and teased him, rubbing herself against him as he watched with glazed-over eyes.

"If I'm dreaming, I hope no one is about to wake me," he said, reaching his fingers toward where they were nearly joined. "God, you're so wet. I need to be in you."

"What are you waiting for?" she said, grabbing his erection and guiding him inside her. They both moaned.

Love Is in the Heir

"This is what I've been waiting for my whole life," he said as he began to move inside her.

"Should've made a move long ago," she said, her breathing becoming tighter as she worked her hips in concert with his, pushing and pulling and hitting that perfect spot that had her near gasping.

"How about we agree to make up for lost time, then?" he said, holding tight to her soft, shapely bottom as he pressed himself deep into her.

"No arguments here," she said as she licked a trail toward his neck and to his ear.

"You've found my weak spot," he said as he rolled her over and spread her legs wide, pressing farther in. He leaned forward with his lips and caught her nipple in his mouth and sucked hard as he pumped faster.

"God, Toph," Pippa shouted as she saw stars and lost her breath, coming hard just as Topher groaned loudly and held himself inside her, pulsing as he released in a warm gush.

Topher sprawled on top of her as they both lay in silence for a minute, catching their breath.

"Holy crap," she said, exhaling loudly. "That was so not what I expected when I showed up at this wedding today."

Topher rolled over and grinned. "Hope you got your money's worth. After all, you did miss the wedding cake."

"Oh, I think I got a way better dessert," she said, her finger trailing along his chest. "Lot less calories too."

"Well, if you're looking for a workout, you've come to the right man," he said as he leaned toward her and kissed her.

"Maybe you'll need to test my stamina a bit more," she

Jenny Gardiner

said with a wink.
"We've got all night."

Chapter Four

PIPPA opened one bleary eye as a bright pinpoint of sunlight sneaking through a gap in the closed draperies practically blinded her. She squinted and took a quick accounting of where she was, and her eyes settled on the beautiful naked chest of His Royal Highness Prince Christopher, Duke of Esmeralda, a man who until twelve hours ago she had presumed she'd never speak more than a handful of words to ever. Who'd suddenly and somewhat bizarrely become a man who'd practically spent the better part of the night buried inside her body.

She so could not process the concept. This was Zander's brother! Zander's brother, whose sexual fantasies had apparently centered around Pippa for years, unbeknownst to her. What was the protocol on this going forward? Would this remain their little secret? One little one-night stand—correction: one *big* one-night stand—with Topher, who'd grown into quite the handsome and virile young man? Not that she'd had a whole lot of experience with this, but he sure seemed to stay, uh, up for quite a long while. At one point last night she'd wondered if maybe this was his superpower: heroic sexual stamina. In which case she was gonna be sore for a week.

Surely there would be no future for the two of them. No way could Topher live down the Wanker thing with her doing the wanking.

Oh, God, she thought. What do I do?

She was torn. She peered down to where the sheet was

draped ever so barely across his hips, right at that sexy juncture where you can tell who's been doing the ab workout or not. Clearly Topher had, cut as he was, and she couldn't help but stare in quasi longing, her eyes following that happy trail of hair that disappeared beneath the sheet. All she needed to do was pull the sheet back just an inch, if that. Which would mean that she was signing up for round what? Six? Eight? Ten? She had lost count hours ago. But if she opted for the command performance route, that would mean she'd of course have to face Toph and actually discuss this dilemma with him. The touching him part, she'd do that in a heartbeat. She knew from the past several hours that would be great fun.

But the talking part? That's where Pippa just couldn't handle it. She knew that having her name attached romantically to Topher's could only mean trouble, and the last thing she wanted to do to the poor guy was resurrect all that old nonsense. She decided to just look at this experience as a lovely way to close some old wounds while also finally getting laid—and enjoying it!

She had no idea what time it was, but judging by the bright sunlight coming through that crack in the curtain, morning had broken long ago. Which meant she was going to have a hell of a time slipping out of a palace in an evening gown.

Shit. Shit shit shit shit shit shit shit shit.

Pippa closed her eyes for a minute. *Breathe*, she told herself. *Just breathe*. In through the nose, out through the mouth. Don't start thinking about the what-ifs and repercussions of what you've done. Just think about how to sneak out discreetly.

With that, she ever so slowly rolled away from Topher,

Love Is in the Heir

barely missing falling to the floor. She backed carefully and quietly out of his bedroom, through the open living room, hoping he didn't have some butler who was going to jump out and find her stark naked trying to escape.

She finally got to the door where her ball gown had fallen unceremoniously into a pile and pulled the thing over her head, tugging the side zipper up. A cursory glance around yielded her elegant Swarovski crystal heels and matching purse, which held her car keys, essential in this getaway plan. She scanned the room in search of her thong, but the thing was nowhere to be found. Finally, she decided to not worry about that and skedaddle.

As she turned the handle on the large front door, she hoped like hell he hadn't set an alarm when he closed it last night; she couldn't imagine the embarrassment that would come from that. She knew in a house with three young men there had been plenty of walks of shame out of this place in the morning. But usually women were probably smart enough to slip out under cover of darkness in the predawn hours. She could only hope people were nursing hangovers from the wedding and rolling over in bed, their pillows shading their eyes.

She tiptoed backward as she drew the door shut and turned around just in time to run up against Luca, the youngest of the brothers.

"Oof!" Pippa said as she bumped into him, trying to remain as quiet as possible.

"Pippa?" Luca said, looking her up and down, with her melon gown a wrinkled mess.

She was sure her mascara had smeared all over her face, and her helter-skelter hair must've looked like she'd stuck a finger in an electrical socket.

"Luca! You scared the crap out of me!"

"Me? How about you?" he said. "Here I am getting ready to go out for a run, and instead I run into you. Did you shut down the wedding or something?" He pointed at her formal wear.

Pippa stalled for time. What excuse could she have for leaving the palace at this hour in her night-before clothes?

"I had way too much to drink," she said, dope slapping her forehead with the heel of her hand. "I just crashed on Zander's sofa."

Luca looked puzzled. "Oh really?"

"Yeah, it was so easy to do that."

"I'm just surprised," Luca said.

"Why?"

"Well, with Andi here, I wouldn't have thought Zander would want anyone else in his apartment, what with making up for lost time and all."

Andi. Dammit. She'd forgotten all about that.

"Did I say Zander? I meant Topher," she said. "See, I must still be drunk. What a stupid mistake!"

Luca knit his brow. "You stayed in Topher's place?"

"So?"

"It's just that, well, you know."

"Oh, come off it, Luca. That was a long time ago. You boys need to stop teasing him about that. It's nothing the rest of you haven't done a million times around here."

Luca rolled his eyes. "I just mean I thought Topher wouldn't even look at you most of the time."

"Well, I guess he's grown up enough to let bygones be bygones and keep a family friend from driving when she was in no condition to get behind the wheel. But I must be going now. Have a great run!"

Love Is in the Heir

With that she scurried off like a mouse trying to avoid detection by the house feline. She only ran into two security guards and three maids as she slipped out the servant's entrance. All in all, it could have been worse. Way worse.

Chapter Five

TOPHER awoke with a smile on his lips, memories of the past several hours swirling through his brain. He reached down to scratch himself and maybe tamp down that ubiquitous morning boner that really shouldn't have needed tending to after the workout that thing had been through.

He rolled over and opened his eyes, fully expecting to find a sleep-tousled Pippa naked and waiting beside him. But there was no Pippa in his bed. He got up, rubbed his belly, pulled on a pair of boxers, and wandered toward the front of the apartment, hoping he'd find her enjoying an espresso in the kitchen. But not only was there no smell of espresso, there was no Pippa, no evening gown in a heap by the front door, nothing.

Goddammit. It really ticked him off she'd pulled a runner. He'd thought better of her, never expecting her to be a coward and bail. They'd had an amazing night together; he never knew he could fit so many challenging positions into a few short hours, but they'd managed it.

Now what?

He walked over to a remote control and pushed a button that opened the curtains, letting a flood of sunlight into the room. He stood with his hands on his hips, surveying the damage. Before they had made it to his bedroom, they'd managed to do it on the cold Carrera marble in the foyer, atop the antique Turkish rug in front of the fireplace (which he'd apparently turned on and forgotten to turn off last night), on the custom-made

Love Is in the Heir

Holstein hair-on-hide leather sofa (that ended up being a little scratchy against his naked behind), and on the dining room table that could accommodate a dinner party of twenty. Topher had enjoyed his own little feast there, and his mouth watered at the memory.

He moved through the apartment, straightening out the various pieces of furniture and artwork that might have been shifted in their zeal last night. It was only then that he found an electric blue thong dangling from an orchid plant. He plucked the panties off the flower, brought them up to his face, and inhaled. Damn. So close, yet so far. He had no idea how he was going to persuade Pippa that a command performance would be in order before he returned to his studies abroad.

He plunked himself onto the black-and-white sofa, his legs spread wide as he twirled the lacy undies around on the tip of his finger, trying to contemplate his options. But none came to mind. Seemed his mind was freeze-framed on the many things he either hadn't gotten around to with Pippa or wanted to do yet again, none of which would be possible if she retreated like a scared cat.

He gave up trying to figure out the mysteries of women and decided to grab a quick shower before departing for the wedding brunch. If you asked him, this wedding thing had overstayed its welcome.

He should've known better than to show up at the brunch after disappearing early from the wedding the night before. As he entered the ballroom, guests milled about in business attire, the women in those silly hats and the men in crisp bespoke suits. Waitstaff passed around flutes of champagne, naturally, but Topher needed something a little more gut busting.

"I'll take a bloody, extra hot sauce," he told a nearby bartender.

Topher stirred the cocktail with a celery stick and took two large swigs of his spicy drink, bracing himself for whatever curveballs his brothers might want to throw his way.

"Well, good morning, sunshine," Zander said as his brother approached the group of them, all gathered in a corner, rehashing the night's events.

Topher gave him a cursory nod and kept himself busy with that bloody.

"You disappeared early last night," Zander continued. "I saw you out on the dance floor, and next thing I knew, you were gone."

"I didn't know you were my keeper," Topher said.

"Whoa, a little sensitive this morning, bro?" Zander said, holding his hands up in surrender.

Squinting his eyes, Topher threw him an annoyed look. "No. Just didn't know I had to answer to you about my whereabouts is all."

"What was most interesting," Zander said to his audience, which included Andi, Darcy, Caroline, Clementine, and Luca, "was who you were cheek to cheek with last night."

Topher glared. "Don't go there, Zander."

"So sensitive," his brother said. "Can't take a little poking some fun at you?"

"Z—"

"I mean if my eyes didn't deceive me, I could swear

Love Is in the Heir

you were mighty close to the divine Miss P," Zander said with a wink.

"Look, I felt sorry for her," Topher said. "She was alone in a corner and everyone was off dancing, so I offered to dance. Nothing more."

"That's funny," Luca said. "Because I saw her leaving your apartment this morning, Toph. She was still in her ball gown, which looked pretty wrinkled."

"Womp," Zander said, clapping his hands. "Don't tell me Pips finally got a good hard look at that good hard—"

Andi elbowed Zander in the gut. "Zander, I don't think your brother wants to discuss this."

Topher decided right there and then he really liked Andi, even though he'd never understand why she was going to settle for his brother.

"I'm just yanking him around," Zander said. "Sort of like what Pippa caught Topher doing to himself that time—"

"Come to think of it, Pips told me she'd stayed at *your* place, Zander," Luca said. "But then I suggested that would be odd, figuring you'd be all about banging a certain someone."

Andi blushed. She had no experience hanging around a bunch of guys who loved to dick on each other.

"There was no banging going on," Zander said, correcting his brother. "We were making love." He fluttered his eyelashes jokingly. Andi ribbed him again with the elbow.

"Zander, you are being so obnoxious!" she said.

"Just a little brotherly love," he said. "But seriously, Pippa said she was in my place? I can promise you that didn't happen last night."

"No. You see, then she changed her story and said that she stayed in Toph's apartment."

Topher hemmed and hawed. "She wasn't feeling well, so I offered for her to come to my place and lie down."

"Oh, so you shared a bed then?" Luca asked.

"No!" Topher said. "I let her sleep in my bed, and I took the sofa."

Luca crossed his arms, scratching his chin with his hand.

"Interesting…," he said, his gaze traveling between Zander and Topher.

"What?" Topher said.

"Pippa told me *she* slept on your sofa. And she said it was because she was drunk."

D'oh. Topher mentally kicked himself for that simple gaff. Although technically she *was* on his sofa for a while.

"So let me get this straight," Zander said, drumming his fingers against his biceps. "Luca here finds Pippa in a walk of shame this morning, coming from our boy Toph's apartment. Pips says she slept on the couch because she was drunk. But then Topher claims he generously gave up his bed for Pippa, who wasn't feeling well, and *he* slept on the sofa."

Topher gritted his teeth while Zander and Luca sized up the situation, walking around their brother as if he were Exhibit A in a murder trial.

Zander pulled out his phone. "That's it. I'm calling Pippa," he said, scratching his chin. "But wait a minute. Shouldn't she be here?"

Topher tried to grab Zander's phone. "Leave her out of this, Z."

Zander called but got no answer, so he left an

Love Is in the Heir

annoying message, then resorted to texting her, reading aloud just to dig the knife deeper for his poor brother.

All right, Pips. We're besties, he typed. Time to fess up. Tell Zander what happened last night. If you own up to it, the punishment will be less severe.

His brother rolled his eyes. "I swear to God you haven't gotten past grade school in emotional maturity."

"Aww, come on, Toph. Just having a little fun with you." Zander punched him in the arm.

"Z, maybe it's time to let up on your brother," Darcy said.

"This is history in the making, Darce," he said. "*The Wank* has come full circle. Inquiring minds want to know details."

Topher walked right up to his brother and rested a hand on each of his shoulders. "Zander, I'm not going to say this again. Shut the ever-loving fuck up. You got it? This is none of your business. And I'm sick and tired of your dicking on me about something I did with my dick practically half my life ago. Something you've done three times a day and then some with your own. *Basta*! Enough!" he said, waving his hand in the air with a flourish.

With that, he turned and walked out of the brunch, returned to his apartment, packed up his things, and got the first flight bound for the Caribbean.

Chapter Six

PIPPA played back Zander's voice mail again, steaming mad. She'd listened to it far too many times, and each time it just infuriated her more. Even though he was one of her best friends, sometimes he really pissed her off when he decided he wanted to push someone's buttons. And he'd pushed them for her, no doubt about it, and she was certain he'd messed with Topher's buttons even more so.

It had been a week since that fateful night, and she had no idea where Topher had gone, nor did she dare pursue this matter with anyone in the royal family. The last thing she wanted was to be grilled about what had happened between her and Topher. She'd rather just replay it in the privacy of her own head, all the while wondering if she'd made a huge mistake by slipping away like a coward. Never in her life had she felt the way she had during those few short hours she'd spent with Topher. But she sure didn't want to open the man up to a lifetime of merciless taunts just because she'd had a quick fling with him.

Since then, Pippa had maintained a low profile, really not wanting to be pulled into the drama she knew was lurking just on the horizon. Until she got sick of being holed up in her house and reached out to her good friend Clementine Squires-Thornton, who agreed to meet up for drinks.

The weather had turned decidedly autumnal, with a slight chill in the air, but nevertheless they opted to savor one of the few remaining days left in the season on an

Love Is in the Heir

outside terrace overlooking the ocean.

"Before you know it, we'll be cozying up in front of fireplaces and planning our ski holidays," Clementine said, rubbing her goose-bumped arms before finally relenting and putting on a bright blue cashmere sweater she'd brought with her.

"I know, right? I'm not ready for this glorious weather to end," Pippa said. "Though I'm a complete sucker for autumn, with changing leaves and the grape and olive harvests."

I'm a sucker for the wine that comes from the grape harvest."

Pippa nodded. "Amen to that."

Their server brought them their much-awaited bottle of red and poured two glasses.

"To the power of the grape," Pippa said, tipping her glass to her friend's.

"Speaking of powerful grapes, were you so drunk at Adrian's wedding that you had to crash on Topher's sofa, or were you so horny you had to share his bed?"

Pippa sputtered out her wine. "You know you're turning this into the grapes of *my* wrath?" she said, wiping her mouth and the tabletop with a napkin. "Nothing like setting aside propriety and getting down to business!"

"Yeah, yeah, I know. But truly, Pips, it's time to fess up. I'm sure it comes as no surprise to you that rumors have been swirling about what went on that night. And it didn't help matters that you failed to show up at the wedding brunch the next day. Man, you should have seen those brothers go at it. I don't think I've ever seen Topher stand up to Zander like that before."

She wanted to feign indifference, but she could no

sooner do that than stop herself from sleeping with the man in the first place. "Like what kind of rumors?"

Clementine started enumerating on her hand, thumb first. "Oh, that you walked in on Topher again in midwank."

Pippa rolled her eyes. "Are people really that idiotic?"

Clementine shrugged. "I'm not saying I believe them, I'm just telling you what I've heard. Consider me the *vox populi*."

"Ugh. The *vox populi* is pissing me off," Pippa said with a grumble. "Besides, you are not the voice of the people. So what else are they gossiping about?"

Clem started again with the finger count. "Well, so we have the 'you bust him masturbating' rumor. Then there is the 'Zander caught the two of you going at it' rumor," she said, straightening her pointer finger.

"Oh my God, people! There was a wedding reception going on. Does everyone think the thing devolved into a weird orgy?"

"I think it's so romantic," Clementine said.

"What's so romantic?"

"Whatever happened!"

"Well, what if nothing happened? Or what if what happened was Topher pushed me out of a window? Would you find that romantic?"

"Oh stop, Pips! You know that didn't happen!"

"I'm just saying all this speculation is making me nuts!"

"Okay, so other rumors," she said as she pulled her middle finger straight to continue counting. "That you and Topher made mad, passionate love, and then you got in a huge fight and he hopped the palace jet and fled the country, enraged."

"Have people lost every last cell in their brains over the past few days? Or were they always this completely daft?"

"Don't shoot the messenger, Pippa. I'm just recounting the gossip I've been privy to."

"Where do you hang out—at the psych ward? All right. What else are these nosy people saying about me that isn't true?"

"That you're pregnant with Topher's baby." She extended her pinky finger for emphasis.

Pippa dipped her head low and kind of half rolled her gaze upward and gave her one of those hard stares. "It's been a week, Clem. A *week*. Do you know the life cycle of a zygote? I mean the stupid thing would barely have gone through mitosis by now!"

"Please tell me you used protection."

"Protection? What the hell am I going to protect him from? I haven't been with a man in forever!"

"Well, what about him?" Clem said. "If he's anything like Zander—"

"Good God, let's hope not. I'm trusting that no one is in Zander's realm of sexual experience. Besides, the man lives alone on a boat half the time. I think his sleeping with me gave his wrist a break from the risk of carpal tunnel syndrome."

Clementine burst out laughing. "Okay, that image makes me want to pee my pants with laughter."

"Poor, poor Topher. The guy didn't do anything different from any of his brothers, I'm sure. And they probably do it on a far-too-regular basis, for that matter. He just had the bad misfortune of me happening upon it."

"Yeah, but you're the one reinforcing it with the carpal-tunnel-syndrome joke."

Pippa looked at her with stern eyes. "I'm serious about that! I mean what else would you do if you were bobbing on a boat with no companionship?"

"If this boat's a rockin', don't come a-knockin'—"

"Yeah, unless you want to wander in on poor Topher taking care of business."

"I don't know. Sounds like from what you said when that happened, he might well be worth walking in on."

Pippa looked sheepish and faux gulped. "Actually…"

"I know, I know. He's packing. Just like the rest of those boys, if rumors are true about them."

Pippa just nodded and took a swig of her wine. "You know I'm not one to feed rumors, but… I had no idea! I mean it's been a good decade since I saw that thing, and I sure don't remember it being quite so girthsome."

"Girthsome? Is that a word?"

They both giggled. "If it's not, it should be," Pippa said. She held up her hand and made a huge circle with her thumbs and pointer fingers.

"Oh shut up," Clem said, swatting her hand at the finger circle. "No way is it that big."

"I'm serious. He's got some impressiveness going on there."

"Next time, I want you to take a picture of it just to prove it to me."

Pippa's eyes grew large. "Oh definitely. I'd make him stop everything so I could just get off a few snapshots of the thing," she said. "But seriously, Clem—next time? Are you mad? I'm not going down that path anymore. I've sworn off Topher or anyone of blood relation to that man.

Love Is in the Heir

I can't bear the idea of Zander and company just laughing their asses off at this strange turn of events. I can totally see Z, leaning up against a pool table, a cold beer sticking out of his shirt pocket—because who else does that but Zander?

"He'd take a swig of that beer and bellow, 'It's come full circle, mates. The Wank is back to where it's begun.' Or some such nonsense. I dearly love Zander, but I also want to throttle the man. Do you think I could do that without going to jail?"

"Maybe you just need to get away for a while, Pips. Put things in perspective. I mean honestly, I think you're overthinking this. So you saw the guy masturbating when he was a teenager. No big deal. And then all of a sudden you end up hooking up with him. And you have a great time. And he's got girthiness, which evidently is something to treasure or covet or at the very least want more of. If I were you, hon, I'd go find me some more girth. But that's just me. I know you. You'll go off and do some do-goody thing and make others less fortunate feel better about their lives. Which is fine. So then go—do it. Stop dwelling on the Episode. But in the meantime… tell me more about what happened!"

By the time they were on their third glass of wine, Pippa was telling her friend how they made their way from the bovine couch to the bedroom.

"God, Pippa, I never thought about little Topher as a sexual being," Clem said. "But damn, he sounds like he knows what he's doing with that thing."

Pippa nodded. "And then some. It was pretty amazing."

"So then after all that, what happened?"

Pippa sighed, pushing her lower lip out in a pout. "I panicked. I woke up, and he was naked, and God, I was so close to just pulling the sheets away and ringing the bell for round six, but then I thought about Zander and how brutal he would be with Topher. Plus I was naked in the palace and it was daylight. Do you have any idea how impossible it is to sneak out of a palace in your night-before clothes? I just freaked, grabbed my things, and left pronto."

"And you didn't say a word to Topher? No note? Nothing?"

Pippa shrugged. "I know, I know. Totally lame of me. I don't know what came over me but for seriously intense panic."

"Wow, to go from high to low like that in a matter of hours."

"You're not kidding."

"And you haven't reached out to him or anything?"

Pippa shook her head. "I don't even have his contact information. What am I supposed to do—ask Zander? Can you imagine the response that would elicit?"

"Well, that's nuts," Clem said. "We could get his number lickety-split. All you have to do is ask me for a little help."

"Yeah, but what's the point? I mean there is no future in anything with Toph and me," Pippa said. "For one thing, he lives far, far away. For another, well, you know the deal. We have a history that is irrevocable."

Clementine waved her hand at her friend. "Oh nonsense. Those are total smoke screens. First of all, do

Love Is in the Heir

you or do you not travel all over the place for work? As in surely you can divert yourself to some stopping point where the two of you could, uh, pick up where you left off," she said, holding her fingers in air quotes. "And for another thing, that whole history excuse is just that: history. You're both grown-ups now! You can't let your life be defined by something that happened when you were teenagers!"

She buried her face in her hands. "I don't know what to do, Clem. I'm too scared to try that. But I'm also sad that I'm such a weenie. I wish we'd had a chance to pursue this more. But now what do I do?"

"Leave it up to your best friend Clem, my dear. I'll work my magic, and before you know it, you'll be on the road to girthdom." She made a huge circle with her fingers.

The two of them broke out in peals of laughter as Pippa ordered some more wine; she knew she was going to need it.

Chapter Seven

TOPHER lifted off his dive mask and scaled the metal ladder into the back of the catamaran he called home. He peeled off his wet suit and hosed off under the outdoor shower nozzle beneath the setting sun just as Sebastian, his skipper, who also happened to be his cousin, handed him a cold beer.

"You're a good man," Topher said, lifting his bottle to him. "Only thing better than a cold beer would've been—"

"A warm snatch," Sebastian said.

They both laughed.

"You must be a mind reader," Topher said. "Although I was trying not to go there in my head, thanks."

"But Your Highness, you can have the pick of the litter. You should never go without."

Topher rolled his eyes. "Stop with the formalities. Besides, you know I'm not like my brother Zander. I don't sleep with women just because I can."

"Then you're a fool," Sebastian said with a belly laugh.

Topher shrugged. "You got me there. It sucks having a conscience."

Truth was, since he'd returned to the British Virgin Islands, he'd thought about only one woman, so much so that he really wished he could clear her out of his head.

But no such luck. Whether he was swimming with sea turtles or measuring coral stress or assessing pollution levels, he still couldn't get Pippa out of his mind. And maybe Pippa would laugh about that, knowing that while he was pondering dirty things, he was thinking of her.

It kind of made him frustrated, because up until now, he'd always been most at peace beneath the surface of these crystalline waters, mesmerized by the movements of a prehistoric-looking Hawksbill turtle or simply fascinated by the behavior of a nearby school of rainbow-colored fish. But now he could barely focus on this underwater nirvana. All because he was suddenly horny. Or was it more than that? It was weird because he'd pined for Pippa for all those years, but when he finally moved away, so did thoughts of her for a very long time. Only to come rushing back upon being near her again, further nurtured by the memories of what it felt like to be inside her, to be kissing her, to be curled up beside her as she softly slept.

"Jesus," he muttered. "I'm not living in a damned romance novel."

Sebastian looked at him and squinted. "You say something?"

Topher shook his head. "Ignore me. My head's all messed up."

"Which one?" he said with a wink.

Toph nodded. "Guilty as charged. Not sure which head is more messed up right now, to be honest."

Sebastian flicked a wet towel toward his friend's crotch. "It's easiest if that's the screwed-up one, because all it takes is an hour with a bird to fix it," he said, then tapped Topher's head. "If it's this head, then you're pretty much out of luck."

The two men laughed, only Topher was really just half laughing, since he knew his buddy was spot-on.

"Here I am in my happy place, and it's keeping me from feeling particularly happy," Topher said. "And the thing of it is I didn't ask for it. I was going on, minding my own business, when she just sort of fell into my lap. And how amazing it was when she was in my lap… But then just as quickly she disappeared."

"It's how they do it," Sebastian said, scratching the two-day beard growth on his chin. The two of them never bothered to shave much while out on the boat. "You just need to figure out how to toughen up and move on. The way I see it, they're a dime a dozen. The best policy is to love the one you're with."

Topher knit his brows and looked at Sebastian. "God, I hope that's not a proposition."

Sebastian roared with laughter. "I'd no sooner settle for you than the man on the moon," he said. "At least the man on the moon's got something to offer me."

Topher crooked an eyebrow. "Oh yeah? Like what?"

Sebastian looked skyward as the moon began to climb the early night sky. "If you look closely, it looks as if there are some holes in it. Give me a hole, and I can make use of it."

Toph shook his head. "I'm not gonna touch that one with a ten-foot pole."

"And likewise with you, mate!"

The two men prepared a meal of grilled spiny Caribbean lobsters along with a salad. Just as they were finishing it up, Topher heard his text message ding, which was strange, as he rarely heard from anyone when he was out here.

He grabbed his phone and opened it up to a text from

an unrecognizable number, though one from back home. For a minute he got his hopes up, only to realize it was Clementine.

Hey Toph! What is up with you? You're probably wondering why I'm texting you when you're clear across the ocean on God-knows-what-island. I can't even begin to guess where you are! Where are you? Anyhow, you don't have to answer that if you don't want to. But I thought I'd participate in a little subterfuge on your behalf.

Topher's brow scrunched up out of concern, wondering what in the hell Adrian's valet, who just happened to be Darcy's sister, was doing contacting him. Sure they'd been friends over the years, but not the kind who would reach out across an ocean just to say "hi."

So I was just chatting with a mutual friend today... You might know who I'm talking about—she's super cute, curly brown hair, hazel eyes. And, well, she didn't tell me everything, but she did tell me enough... Oh, but I am sworn to secrecy, so I won't tell you what she told me. So I won't even tell you if I now know for a fact if that rumor about the royal brothers is true. Hee hee! Just joking! Or maybe I'm not!

He rolled his eyes. A while back, his brother Adrian had been exposed as having a particularly large, uh, package. Seems when he was being fitted for some fashion event in Milan—a fundraiser for one of his father's charities—the men in charge of being sure his pants fit "just so" went public with how very snugly they did fit. Poor Adrian was fit... to be tied, that is.

And Zander, well, Zander had his own way of broadcasting his gifts, by stripping naked in a Vegas swimming pool and having his assets displayed in tabloids the world over. From then on, the cocks of the Monafortian princes had become the stuff of lore. Nothing like a little crass objectification. But the way Topher saw it, if men could do it to women, then they too ought to be fair game. Besides, at least they weren't known for being particularly diminutive. That would definitely be worse, at least from their perspective.

So anyhow, as I said, I had drinks with Pips, and I have to tell you, Toph, I think she's got the hots for you. I've never seen Pippa so distracted before. And I think she was sort of depressed now that you're gone. I know she questioned if what she did was stupid. But I think she thinks she was doing you a big favor. Even though I tried to tell her she'd be doing you a bigger favor if she hadn't dumped you like that. But you know how stubborn Pippa can be. So I just wanted to let you know I've got your back on this one, because I have Pip's back, and I want this to work for her because I think she really does as well, if only she'd admit it. I haven't quite figured out how I'm going to orchestrate this, but trust me. It's on my to-do list.

Topher heaved a sigh. Clearly there was no question but that whatever happened had become public knowledge. Which meant he'd made the right decision to get far away from all that nonsense. If only getting far from it didn't mean being so far from the woman at the center of this whole mess. He wasn't quite sure what to say to Clementine, but he needed to acknowledge that he got her message at least, so he started to type.

Well, I sure didn't expect to have you hunt me down in the middle of the ocean. I suppose the world's smaller than we all think. I guess you're in on my secret. Hopefully not you and all Monaforte. Though I trust by now it's been broadcast far and wide. God forbid I ever get away from stupid things that happened half a lifetime ago.

He took a deep breath.

I don't know why Pippa left. You probably know better than me. I wish we'd had a chance to talk some more. But that wasn't going to happen. Then I just couldn't put up with all the nonsense from my brothers, so I decided to come back here right away. I don't have to put up with all the family dynamics when I'm out here, and that's fine by me. If only I could get Pippa out here too, it would be just about perfect. So feel free to work your charms on her. I'm sure I'd in no way be persuasive with her, so perhaps you're my only chance. There's a grilled Anageda lobster in it for you, eaten on the stern of a forty-foot catamaran while floating in the calm waters of Drake Channel.

Of course, if he was to treat her to a lobster dinner on the back of the sailboat, that would mean Clementine would be here, which would be a little hairy if he actually had Pippa here as well. Not exactly easy to find privacy on a boat the size of a tennis court.

Chapter Eight

CLEMENTINE had struggled earlier in the year, as her father had passed away unexpectedly. It had been a tough several months, and so it was with renewed excitement that she hosted a surprise birthday party for her dear friend Pippa.

"Okay guys," she said to the crowd gathered in the large living room of her family's estate. "Thank you all so much for coming. Pip's gonna absolutely freak out when she shows up and we all scare the crap out of her. So I need you guys to be completely silent when she pulls up. It's going to be so awesome."

As she worked her way through the crowd, she bumped into Zander, who stood in a corner with his hands all over his officially Very Serious Girlfriend Andi, who as an unexpected guest at Adrian's wedding had made her debut as Zander's significant other.

"Z, so glad to see you know what to do with those hands," Clementine said, razzing him. "Here I thought you only knew how to use them on yourself."

Zander fake laughed. "In deference to your emotional state over the past however many months, I'll pretend you didn't say that," he said. "Although have you ever considered a career as a comedian?"

"Aww, Zander, you know I love you. Just giving you a taste of your own medicine is all," Clementine said. "And a segue into my warning you not to say anything that is going to upset Pippa. I think she's still furious with you, and it

Love Is in the Heir

was a risk I chose to take including you on the guest list tonight. Which means you have an unwritten social contract with me to keep your mouth shut. Got it?"

She then extended her hand out to Andi. "Hi! I know we met at the wedding, but it was all a blur," she said. "I'm so happy you've finally tamed the beast. You'll find him to be irrepressibly charming yet sometimes confoundingly irritating."

"All the above and then some," Andi said with a broad smile as she shook Clem's hand. "Of course I remember you, and thanks for the warning. I've also read the riot act to Zander so that he doesn't upset Pippa tonight. He's sworn to be on his best behavior."

"More like she threatened to cut me off if I said anything."

"Whatever it takes, Alexander," Clem said. Then she pointed at her eyes with two fingers then one at him. "I'm watching you, buddy."

Zander spread his hand and jokingly put his palm toward Clementine's face to push her away.

"I think I hear the caterers calling for you," he said, cupping his ear with his hand as if listening through the din of the crowd.

Pippa just did not want to go out. It had rained all day, and the humidity did nothing for her hair, so once again she pulled it back into her trademark braid, but spare bits of it escaped the attempt at taming and frizzled around her face as if zapped by a bolt of lightning. After trying to tamp them down for a few minutes, she gave up, threw on a threadbare pair of jeans and her dingiest old sweater, spurning even the simplest application of makeup, and hopped in her car. She'd given strong thought to showing up in her pajamas; she was that not into going out into this cold, dreary night.

But she'd promised Clementine she'd show up at her house to hang out with her tonight. She was trying to be mindful of Clem's feelings, since she'd lost her father several months earlier. It seemed that Clem would start to feel better, only for something to trigger her sadness and grief again, so Pippa had become adept at anticipating when Clementine might need some companionship. And a dreary, wet autumn evening alone at home could be just the ticket.

She'd have loved nothing better than to call Zander to come watch a movie in her home theater, like old times. Except she was still not speaking to him, and it felt sort of lonely to do so by herself. Her parents had been gone for months now on one of those luxury cruises around the world—they had their very own penthouse apartment on an elegantly appointed cruise ship, where they got on and off at their leisure.

They'd not be home for another six months, which meant a lot of solitary nights had been accruing for Pippa. Not that she felt a need to live alongside her parents at this point in her life, but being in a big old house on her own just got sort of depressing after a while. Which is why she acceded to Clem's wishes and drove to her family's estate; it was only about twenty minutes from her place but felt like it was hours away. What with the heavy rain coming down and her wiper blades barely keeping up with it, it seemed like she'd been driving all night. She couldn't decide what

Love Is in the Heir

was coming down harder, the rain or leaves being blown from the trees with the storm. Either way, it made for a stressful trek.

She pulled up to the house and got out of her car only to end up with one foot ankle-deep in mud.

"This is just bloody perfect," she said, muttering. "She had better have some damned good wine at the ready."

She shook off the spare mud from her foot, trying to wipe the sole of her trainers on the wet grass so she didn't track dirt into the house.

She climbed the steps and rang the doorbell—one of those doorbells that goes on forever. Oddly, no one came to the door. Pippa knocked with the large brass horse-head knocker, a nod to the racehorses Clem's father, Lord Weltenham, had long bred.

"Huh," Pippa said. "Where the hell is she?"

She tried the door latch, and it gave when she pressed down on it, so she went ahead and opened the door. Not that she hadn't regularly helped herself to entering their home in the past, but it seemed weird to do that now that she was a grown-up.

"Clem?" Pippa shouted, confused because the lights were all out. "Where the hell are you? Stop messing with me and get out here. This place is kind of creepy in the dark!"

Just then, the lights went on, and a collective yell of surprise just about sent Pippa to the emergency room with heart failure. She stood there, jaw open, unable to comment.

Finally she spoke. "Are you fucking kidding me?" she said, looking with murderous eyes at Clementine, who was leading the pack.

Clementine reached out and grabbed her arm and pulled her into a two-cheeked kiss. "Surprise?" she said with a laugh as she then gave her friend a once-over.

"My God, you sure do clean up well, Pips," she said, pointing out her left foot, which was mud covered to her ankle, and mentioning the slovenly outfit.

"You said you were *lonely*," Pippa said. "I wanted to stay home and watch a movie. It's miserable out there. Yet I came because you needed me. But then, well, this!" She stretched her arms out to point out the obvious.

"Oh stop with your issues," Clementine said.

"Issues? I practically came over in my pajamas. Besides, on a good day, I'm not one to dress up!"

"Well, hey! At least I got you here. And a good fifty of your closest friends were willing to brave the elements just to help you celebrate!"

"Oh, God, Clem, that was rude of me," Pippa said, apologizing. "I guess you just totally threw me with this surprise, and, well, look at me. I'm a hot mess."

"I'd venture to guess you won't be picking up anyone looking like that tonight."

Pippa tossed her a "shut up" look. "Try ever."

"Oh, I dunno," Clem said. "You never know what's just around the corner."

"Promise me you haven't flown anyone here without my consent."

"Of course not! You know I'd never do something like that," Clem said. "All good, my friend. Now let's get a drink in your hand, and let's get this party started!"

Chapter Nine

THE party was winding down, and Pippa had thankfully managed to pep up for the guests, despite her hangdog attitude earlier that night. She even extended a cursory hello to Zander and warmly greeted Andi.

"Sweetie!" she said to Andi, kissing her cheek twice. "I can't tell you how happy I am to see you here. Even if it is with a certain someone." She rolled her eyes over her continued annoyance with Zander.

"Pips, I wouldn't miss this for anything," Andi said. "You've been so wonderful to me I was happy to come celebrate your birthday. And as far as that certain someone, well, let's just say he's on notice."

"Good," Pippa said. "I'm sure the man only responds to being cut off." She winked again.

"How'd you know that's what I threatened him with?"

"The oldest tool in the book."

Andi shrugged. "Yeah, true dat. But hey, it works."

Pippa smiled.

"I'm still a little irate with Zander, but I'll come around. Eventually. In the meantime, make sure he knows you're in charge."

"Already taken care of," she said. "We're going to take off. I think Zander doesn't want to be hit up for dishwashing duty."

"As if he ever has been!"

"I know, right?" Andi said. "It's more likely that he wants to cash in his reward for good behavior tonight."

"In that case, go." Pippa pushed her friend toward the door. "Someone around here needs to get lucky."

Finally all that remained were Clementine and Pippa. Even Clem's brothers had gone off to bed as had her brother Darcy's fiancée, Caroline.

"Damn, seems like everyone is pairing off these days, doesn't it?" Pippa said with a whiny tone of voice as she helped collect beer bottles and dirty dishes.

"It's not fair," Clementine said. "Why not us?"

Pippa sighed. "Seriously. Leave it to me to find the one person on the planet I wouldn't mind being with but can't," she said. "Not that he'd want to be with me again anyhow."

Clementine shook her head. "I swear you are about as daft as they come, girl."

Pippa knit her brows. "Huh?"

"If you think for one second that Topher doesn't want to be with you, well then you must have been completely high when you were with him and missed out on what actually happened that night."

"That's funny," she said. "I haven't been high since my first year at university. I couldn't tolerate the calorie intake involved with smoking weed, so I gave it up. So I was definitely not high. Besides, how would you know?"

Clem rapped on her head with her knuckles. "Uh, you told me in pretty much graphic detail."

"Me and my big mouth."

"So I have one present I forgot to give you," Clem said, slipping an envelope into her hands.

"What is this?"

"Oh, a little something from me to you," she said. "The thing is, it expires at midnight, so you have to take advantage of it right now."

Love Is in the Heir

"What are you talking about?"

Clementine pointed at the envelope. "Open it!"

Pippa slid her finger along the sealed edge of the envelope and pulled out a sheet of paper inside.

Dear Pippa, it read in Clementine's quite impressive cursive. Surprise! Not only did I totally catch you off-guard with this party, but I also have an even bigger surprise for you! Now go to the front door and look outside.

Pippa scrunched her brows, deeply suspicious about what was up, while Clementine ushered her to the front of the house. She entirely expected a whole 'nother group of friends to shout out "surprise" and give her another near heart attack. But instead, what she saw was a long white limousine with a driver standing next to it holding a sign that read *Pippa Grimaldi*.

"Okay...," Pippa said.

"So here's the deal," Clem said. "I've had a hard time of it over the past several months with losing my father. And you've had a hard time of it over the past couple of months, well, for other reasons. So I decided that you and I are going to get away from it all for a week! Starting now!"

"What?" Pippa said, incredulous.

"There's a plane waiting for us at the airport. I had your maid pack a bag for you, so you're all ready!"

Pippa shook her head, trying to absorb it all. "Like right this second I'm supposed to just set everything aside and go to some mystery destination with you?"

"Well, why the hell not?" Clem said. "I mean have you ever had anything but fun with me? Plus you have no place you have to be. I know that for a fact. I also had Greta look at your calendar on your computer to be sure you had no pressing engagements."

"And here I thought Greta was just a good housekeeper. I had no idea she was a veritable spy."

"Your bag's in the limo already," Clem said. "I'll just grab mine from my bedroom and give my mother a quick kiss, and we'll be off! Oh, and one last thing," she added. "We're flying on a royal jet. I told Zander that he owed it to you for all the trouble he's caused."

"Sometimes I could kill you," Pippa said. "But this time I think I might just squeeze you to death with a hug. Divine retribution makes me happy."

Chapter Ten

IT'S not that Pippa didn't travel in a rarified world; she did, and such things as first-class accommodations were part of her regular travel experience. But there was something amazingly special about flying on one of the Firm's jets, which put even premier class to shame. The Firm was the insider's term referring to the royal family. She had joined Zander's family on many occasions for holidays, so it wasn't her first time in one of their jets. But it was her first time with just her and her best friend. With an entire plane to themselves.

"I don't think I've stayed up all night for a girls' night since I was at boarding school," she said, giddy with excitement. "But I think this calls for endless glasses of champagne and a movie marathon."

"Yes, I'm afraid we have to settle for movies," Clem said. "I thought about arranging for a male stripper, but then you'd be stuck with the man for the entire flight."

They looked at each other, shook their heads, and laughed.

"God, no!" Pippa said. "Happy to settle for eye candy on the big screen."

Because it was late, the flight crew didn't offer up a dinner, but by the time morning arrived, they were treated to a breakfast of ~~belgian~~ Belgian waffles with hot syrup and local sausage from Monaforte.

"I swear I don't think I can stomach any more champagne, but mimosas, well, what can I say?" Pippa said, pointing at the flute placed in front of her.

Clem nodded. "Can't. Turn. Down."

They both tipped their glasses and took a sip, laughing.

"Oh this is the life," Pippa said, "when the biggest care in the world is whether or not you're obligated to drink yet more bubbly."

"I'm all over it," Clem said.

"Okay, so when are you going to tell me where we're going?"

Clementine shook her head. "When we get there! It's a surprise. It wouldn't be much of one if I spoiled it in advance, now would it?"

The women passed the time playing Scrabble and watching more movies until the pilot finally announced they were about to land. Pippa looked out the window to see the most beautiful water she'd ever seen before in competing shades ranging from teal and azure to ultramarine and indigo. It sparkled with reflected sunlight, and every now and again she could see the wind-infused pop of a sail winking at them.

"It's beautiful," she said as she fastened her seat belt, still no clue where they were.

"Okay, now you have to promise me you won't look at any signs though once we land," Clem said. "In fact, I brought a scarf that I'm going to tie across your eyes. This is going to be a big surprise for you."

"Or creepy," Pippa said. "I feel like I'm being kidnapped."

Clem shrugged. "In a way, you are. In the best of ways, that is. But I like to consider it best-friend-napped."

Before getting off the plane, Clementine tied the scarf blindfold around Pippa's head, then helped to guide her

Love Is in the Heir

down the steps of the jet to a waiting car.

"God, it's hot," Pippa said. "You sure I can't take this thing off? It's making my eyeballs sweat!"

"I don't think it's physically possible for eyeballs to sweat. Besides, no negotiating with the hostage taker," Clem said. "Just follow my directions, and everyone will be happy."

Pippa grumbled. "Happy schmappy. I want to know where I am!"

"In due time."

Once they got out of the vehicle, Pippa could smell the scent of brine in the air and knew she was being led toward the water, but for what purpose, she still hadn't a clue. Clem escorted her closer toward the salty scent until she heard a man's voice.

"Ladies," the man said. "Welcome aboard. My name's Sebastian, and I'll be your skipper."

Sebastian took hold of Pippa's hand and shook it, which she thought was awfully strange, considering she couldn't even see him.

Then, with Sebastian holding one elbow and Clementine the other, Pippa was lowered into what she figured was a dinghy.

She heard an engine start, and then they were off, motoring toward who knew where.

Once they were far enough from land to no longer be able to see signage, Clementine removed the blindfold from Pippa's eyes.

"Wow," Pippa said, taking a look at the scenery. As far as she could see, calm seas in every direction, morphing in color from cerulean to aquamarine to seafoam green, were set against a cloudless blue sky. Occasionally in the distance, she'd see islands popping up, with white sugar sand beaches and sleepy palm trees.

"When you decide to kidnap someone, you sure do know how to do it right."

"I'm thinking of starting a business doing this," Clem said.

"I'll reserve judgment on whether I'll give you a good review or not."

"You kidding me?" Clem said. "Honey, I know you're going to give me five stars on TripAdvisor. Just you wait. Right, Sebastian?"

Pippa gave the skipper a once-over. He was surprisingly handsome for a boat captain. Perhaps it was unfair of her to think that, but she always thought of sailor types as sort of rode hard and put up wet, weathered with the weather, as it were. But this Sebastian guy had wind-tousled light brown hair with sun-kissed highlights that framed a face with warm brown eyes and a broad, white smile. She could only hope the skipper was going to be at their disposal. Judging by the sidelong glances Clem was throwing his way, she figured somebody had designs on the man.

Soon the dinghy approached a large catamaran, stark white against the brilliant sea. As they neared the sailboat, Pippa could just make out the name emblazoned on the back of it: *Royal Blue*. A logical sort of name, considering the color of water it was floating on, she thought, but sort of boring. She'd have gone for something a little more creative, like *Fanta-sea*, or *Yacht-Sea* (one of her favorite games when she was young). Or maybe *Sea Sic*. Well, that would be good if you were a writer or editor. Or Latin buff. Back to the drawing board with that one, she thought.

Love Is in the Heir

Lost in thought, Pippa barely noticed when a man wearing a baseball cap appeared at the stern of the boat, standing with hands on hips, waiting to help tie up the dinghy once they got close enough. She didn't have her sunglasses on, thanks to Clementine's earlier blindfold maneuver, so she had to shade her eyes with her hand and squint to see what the man looked like.

With the sun at his back, it was hard to really tell, what with the glare from the late-day sun. His eyes were shaded by a pair of glasses with orange reflective lenses. A little loud, but it worked in this tropical setting. What hair she could see, peeking out from his cap, was wet and slicked back but was decidedly dark. Her gaze continued down the length of him, and her breath hitched.

She'd recognize that chest anywhere; she'd spent enough hours near it, on it, and under it, and with her roaming hands all over the thing (that is, when they weren't a little lower on his torso). Topher. Her eyes grew wide as she realized what her friend had done. She started to stand, but standing doesn't work without some forethought when on a malleable dinghy and she nearly fell overboard.

"Clementine Squires-Thornton," she said, trying to catch her balance, her voice elevated to near shrill. "The minute I'm on terra firma, I am going to absolutely kill you. But before I kill you, I'm going to seriously kill you."

Clem smiled. "Well, good, because it'll be a while till you're on terra firma, so I think I'm safe for now."

"You do not play fair."

"All's fair in love and kidnapping, my friend."

Pippa gritted her teeth. "Whoever said anything about love?" she said with a growl. "For that matter, who said anything about friend?"

She glared at Clementine. She wasn't sure if it was good or bad that the dinghy motor prevented Topher from hearing the gist of the conversation.

"Well, how about lust, then?" Clementine said. She exchanged knowing glances with Sebastian, who'd been staring intently at Clementine's cleavage. "Lust works fine for me."

The dinghy quickly pulled up alongside the sailboat, and Sebastian tossed a rope to Topher to tie up the small boat. Within minutes, Pippa, Clementine, and their duffels were ushered to the back of the boat to the awaiting Topher.

Chapter Eleven

"WELL, hello there," Topher said, leaning in to kiss Pippa's cheek, which she promptly deflected with a quick reach of the hand instead. "We meet again." He shook her hand vigorously, as if he was a politician seeking her vote.

"We 'meet'? Or better yet, 'I've been hoodwinked into being here'?" Pippa said, squinting her eyes.

"Hoodwinked?" Topher said, giving a quick wink to Clementine. "Why, you make it sound like your friend had malicious intent, bringing you here under false pretenses. Shame on her." He wagged his finger in jest at Clementine.

"I didn't say anything about Clem being malicious," Pippa said. "I simply said I was brought here under completely false pretense."

Clementine spread her arms out. "And what a miserable-piece-of-shit place to be dragged to," she said, high-fiving Sebastian at that smarmy crack. "I know if my friend pulled something like that on me, I'd probably hug her."

Pippa shook her head. "You know what I mean, Clem. You didn't tell me the truth because you knew I wouldn't have come."

Clem nodded. "No duh. Which is why you're here! I didn't tell you the truth—so shoot me! Now, let's stop quibbling over semantics, because I want to get my bathing suit on and try out this perfect water."

She grabbed Sebastian's hand and asked him to show her to her room, leaving Topher to escort Pippa down the hatch as well, although Pippa maintained her distance with no intention of any overt body contact of the palm-on-palm (or anything-on-anything) variety.

They descended one by one down the short wooden staircase to the salon.

"Home sweet home," Topher said, spreading his arms wide to show them the "living room." And what a room it was.

The bright living area consisted of a long table of polished burled oak surrounded by plush white leather seat cushions that doubled as living room chairs and overstuffed linen pillows in varying shades of blue. Off to one side was a nice-sized galley kitchen outfitted in white Corian countertops with coordinating oak cabinets. There was a large flat-screen television on one wall.

"This is perfect," Clem said, throwing herself onto the leather seat cushions and resting her feet on the table. "I could get used to this mighty quickly."

"Don't," Pippa said. "We're not going to be on here long enough for that to happen."

Clementine waved her hand past Pippa to motion to Topher for him to ignore her. "She's just got a little agita."

They all smiled but for Pips, who grimaced at her.

"Time's a-wasting," Clem said as she got up again. She pointed to Sebastian. "And how about you take me to my quarters while these two lovebirds swab the deck." She gave a pronounced wink.

Pippa rolled her eyes, knowing that meant she was defaulted to Topher as her boat tour guide.

Topher showed her to her relatively plush cabin, with a queen-sized berth and plenty of drawer space, then even gave her a primer on how to use the downright swanky,

Love Is in the Heir

electric-powered bathroom facilities.

They all met back up in the living room.

"I'll leave snorkeling gear near the ladder because we have some lovely reefs nearby to explore," Topher said. "And if you need anything else, by all means let us know."

"Okay, well, we can tour more later, but I'm getting my suit on," Clementine said, scurrying toward her room. "Last one in has to kiss Topher!"

The three of them laughed, but Pippa just grumbled as she closed the door to her cabin and opened her duffel. In which she found a fat pile of condoms, front and center.

"I am so going to kill you, Clem," she yelled to her.

Pippa was the last one to get into the water, which probably unfairly got Topher's hopes up that she really did want to be the one to have to kiss him. The sight of her in her tiny black bikini was no doubt frustrating the hell out of him. *Good*, thought Pippa. *Serves him right.* Although the sight of his broad sun-kissed chest and lean muscular legs as he floated on his back were taunting her probably just as much. *So much for divine retribution.*

"I'm going off to snorkel," Pippa said, pulling a mask over her face.

"You have to use the buddy system!" Clementine said while treading water next to her. "And my buddy is Sebastian. Sorry, Pips. Looks like you're paired off with Topher." She tapped her on the head with her snorkel.

Pippa took off her mask and glared at Clem. "Remind me to drown you as soon as I get a chance."

"Before you know it, you'll be drowning in your own

sea of love," Clem whispered to her with a subversive wink and gentle elbow to the ribcage.

Pippa growled and pulled her mask back on. "Are you coming?" she asked Topher in a less-than-cordial tone.

She kicked hard with her flippers and set off toward a nearby rocky outcropping with Topher on her heels.

At first Pippa worked hard to pretend she was on her own, not even looking over her shoulder to see if Toph was nearby. She couldn't quite put her finger on why she was being so disagreeable, really. Poor Topher seemed happy to welcome her with open arms, but she had it in her head that this thing needed to be over and done with, and she wasn't going to be part of some juvenile hijinks orchestrated by others that would only serve to perpetuate what she saw as her enormous mistake.

Besides, all that was going to happen was word would get back to the rest of the Family, as the royals were known, and next thing you know their fling would be made a mockery. She didn't need that in her life. Nor did she want to be part of anything that would make it even worse for Topher. Sure he might want her now, but certainly not at the expense of his longer-term dignity.

Once Pippa reached the reef, she lowered her head beneath the surface of the water so she could check out what was swimming around her, and finally her tension started to wash away with the gentle movement of the warm water and the sense of calm that came with the underwater world enveloping her. Topher swam up next to her and occasionally pointed out interesting fish to her. Soon he motioned for her to rise to the surface.

"You see that ugly fish I just pointed out to you?" he said. "It's called a thick-lipped grunt."

Love Is in the Heir

Pippa wondered if he was suggesting perhaps it was a distant relative of hers, what with that surly-sounding name. If he wanted to think she was a grunt, then so be it. But maybe at least not a thick-lipped one.

"How'd he get that charming name?" she said, feigning detachment.

"Oh, there are plenty of grunts: para para grunt, banana grunts, striped grunts, solid ones."

"And are they all particularly grouchy?"

Topher laughed. "Ha! The only *grumps* around here are of the human variety. Actually, they're named for a piglike grunt they make with their throat teeth."

"Very funny," she said. "Whoever's paid the big bucks to put their ear up close to a tiny fish to hear a noise coming from it, I'd like to know."

Topher continued with his fun fish facts. "Some grunts are known for kissing, or at least that's what it looks like, as if they're touching lips. There are grunts called sweetlips, by the way."

Now the normal Pippa, the bawdy, spirited, never-worry-much-about-what-she's-going-to-say-around-the-guys Pippa, would make some crack about a fish with thick lips or one called sweetlips. Probably along the lines of "I bet you'd like to get that fish's lips around your—"

But this quasi-ticked-off, somewhat weirdly bashful version of Pippa that had just materialized in the past hour or so wouldn't dare make suggestive comments to which Topher could retort in a sexually suggestive way because then what would she do? She sure didn't want to set herself up for having to shut him down. Even if she maybe didn't actually want to shut him down.

Luckily he was none the wiser to the self-editing going

on in her confused brain. "Grunts, like young angelfish, are sort of like the coral reef's version of a car wash," he said. "Fish pull up alongside them, and they'll work their magic to clean up the exterior on other fish, picking off parasites, which they feed on." He made a polishing motion with his hand.

"They're the mother baboons of the ocean."

It was actually work for Pippa to pretend to be so disinterested. She was almost getting mad at herself for it but not quite. Amazing what a sense of self-preservation will do to a person. She lowered her mask and began to swim around again. But the minute she saw a very long, shiny silver fish, she squealed and tapped Topher to rise to the surface.

"Oh my God. Is that thing going to eat me?" she asked, holding on to his shoulder.

He shook his head. "It's a tarpon, and he's totally harmless. Though we're harmful to him—fishermen love to go after those things."

"I seriously thought it was a shark."

"You might want to brush up on your shark-recognition skills, 'cause it looks nothing like a shark."

"Well, it is silver."

"So is that necklace you're wearing," he said, pointing to her throat. "Is that a shark? Besides, sharks are gray, not silver."

She smacked his biceps with her hand. "Fine. Whatever. I'm going back under to look some more."

For a while they meandered amidst the coral reef, Pippa at the helm. It was damned near impossible for her to remain in a particularly pissy state of mind, immersed in the tranquil undersea world as she was. Occasionally, she'd

Love Is in the Heir

point to a brightly colored fish or a school of them swirling about and hope that Topher could tell that she wasn't completely rejecting him.

It wasn't until she drifted closer to shore that she realized she was nearly penned in on three sides by reef and rocky outcroppings, and surrounding her everywhere were those ominous-looking, long-spined black sea urchins. Panic set in as her breathing became labored; she had no idea how to get out without being pierced by the venomous spines of the creatures. And with Topher trailing behind her, she had no way to back out. She wanted to cry, but a hell of a lot of good it would do to cry in salt water. Suddenly she felt herself being pulled backward until she finally reached a place where the sea urchins no longer enveloped the area. The water was still shallow enough for her to stand on the tips of her flippers, so she stood and raised her head from the surface, grabbing hold of Topher in a death vise.

"Oh, Toph, I can't believe you saved me from those terrifying things," she said, her breath still coming at a fast clip as if she'd just run for her life. More like swam for her life, only she wasn't actually able to do that. "Thank you for that."

Topher nodded his head. "Not a problem, love," he said. "I saw you'd boxed yourself into a prickly corner and was happy to spare you that misery."

"Do they hurt?"

"*Do they?* Uh, yeah," he said. "Not only does a sting from one of those hurt like hell, but often the spine breaks off in your flesh and you get infected. Not what you'd want during an idyllic Caribbean vacation."

Pippa pondered the idyllic part of that concept. Okay.

Jenny Gardiner

Gorgeous venue. Check. Gorgeous man. Check. Gorgeous boat. Check. Cranky, stubborn Pippa trapped with evil poisonous seagoing creatures. Waaaaaa!

Only then did she realize she was still clinging to Topher for dear life.

"Um, yeah, idyllic," she said, extricating one arm at a time and trying to feign as if she wasn't trying to do just that.

"Kind of like how it felt right then when you had your arms around me," Topher said, placing his hands on her hips and pulling her closer toward him again. But it wasn't going to be an easy task to get those legs around his hips without her raising a fuss, what with those big old flippers on. Especially with an uncooperative witness. And Pippa was wise to his machinations.

"I don't think that's such a good idea, Toph," she said, although she didn't put up much of a struggle, so he kept his hands right where they were.

"And exactly why not?" he asked, raising one hand to the back of her head, pulling her face toward his.

"You know this is just going to cause trouble."

"I love trouble."

"You know what I mean."

"Tell me what you really mean, Pippa, and not what you think you should mean."

"I mean you and I are an impossible match," she said. "It'll only end up getting back to Zander, and then it'll create all sorts of problems. I want no part of that piling on."

"I can think of some piling on you might want to be a part of," Topher said as he grazed his lips against hers.

Pippa shook her head. "Been there, done that, suffered

the aftermath of your brother's mockery."

"Look, Pips, I'm sorry if Zander was being a prick," he said. "You know he'll happily double down on giving you grief since you're practically like family. But in the end, he'll stop. He can't go on like that forever."

"Honestly, *we* can't go on like this forever," she said, pushing away. "Why don't we simply agree to be friends."

She lowered her mask over her face and, with a swift flipper kick, headed into deeper water, leaving what was likely a rather confused and frustrated Topher behind.

Chapter Twelve

BY the time Pippa and Topher got back to the boat, dusk was settling in around them, and their friends were already putting the finishing touches on dinner. Sebastian had soft jazz playing on the speakers, and the whole scene could've been a commercial for the tourism bureau. Or an advertisement for mating. If there was such a thing.

"Well, look at you two lovebirds," Clem said, which earned her a dirty look from Pippa. Topher simply shook his head at her as he toweled off.

"Looks like we've got a stubborn one on our hands," Clem whispered to Toph.

"I'm not deaf, you know," Pippa said as she dropped her snorkeling gear into the storage compartment. "I can hear everything you're saying."

"You're deaf to the poor man's valiant efforts to woo you," Clem said. "I swear I've never seen you so dug in before."

"I don't want to talk about it," Pippa said. "I'm going to get showered."

"Oh, no you're not," said Clem. "No time for that. Dinner is ready now, and we've slaved over a hot galley stove to make this right."

Pippa blew out a breath of indignation. "Fine," she said, wrapping her towel around her as if it were a bath towel. She wasn't particularly keen on dining across the table from Topher in her skimpy bikini top, figuring that would only give him ideas.

Love Is in the Heir

A small table was set on the stern end of the boat, with romantic candles burning. The two of them had grilled lobster and vegetables and cooked up a rice dish as well.

"Good thing they didn't serve us sea urchins," Topher said, leaning his head down to lock eyes with Pippa. His face broke into a wide grin.

"Those things are dreadful," Clem said. "Tried them in Italy one time. Looked like something you'd cough up if you had chronic lung disease."

"All the more reason it's good they're not on the menu tonight then," Sebastian said, rubbing his hands, ready to dig into his lobster. He pointed at Topher and Pippa. "You two have a close encounter of the sea urchin kind?"

Pippa shuddered. "Terrifying," she said. "Those creatures were everywhere!"

"You got trapped by them?" Clem asked.

"I couldn't move! They were on either side of me, in front of me, everywhere!"

"How'd you get out?"

Pippa glanced toward Topher with a sheepish grin.

"A little ocean rescue was in order," Topher said, buffing his nails on his chest as if boasting about his savior prowess.

"He pulled me out by the flippers," Pippa said.

"Awwww, that's so sweet," Clementine said. "Your knight in shining swim trunks."

Pippa rolled her eyes. "Yes, exactly what I was going to say."

"Well, I think it's charming," Clementine said. "He swoops in and saves you just in time. Maybe it's a sign."

"What? That he passed his lifeguard test?"

Clem shook her head. "I don't know what I'm going

to do with you, duchess," she said, bowing with a flourish. "In the meantime, sit down and eat."

Sebastian poured wine for them all as they found their seats; then he raised his glass. "To friends, both old," he said, nodding toward Pippa and Topher, then turning his gaze toward Clementine, "and new. May they be everlasting."

Pippa took a few sips of her wine and soon found herself loosening up a bit. And as she tackled her lobster, she finally started allowing herself to have fun.

"This is actually quite amazing," she said, looking around as the last of the sun set on the horizon, bathing the few clouds in the sky in purple light. "How is it that you get to live in such a perfect place?"

"It didn't take much persuading after my first trip here," Topher said. "And once I talked Sebastian into bringing his boat down here, I mean who couldn't survive in this tropical paradise?"

Sebastian nodded. "Toph knew I was bumming around in tropical ports, and he promised me I'd fall in love with the place," he said. "I ended up here three years ago and never looked back."

"How do you two know each other?" Clem asked.

"We're cousins," Topher said. "Our mums are sisters, only his is much younger than mine."

"And far less powerful," Sebastian said with a grin. "Thank God."

"Sounds like there's more to that story," Clem said.

"Aha!" Pippa said. "Now I remember you. I think we met one Christmas when you were like five years old. Wasn't there some battle over who got to keep the children when your parents split up? And you spent the holidays

Love Is in the Heir

with the Firm?"

"Yeah, well, suffice it to say my parents were far too busy burying the dagger in each other's backs to take on the responsibility of running a country, let alone a family. It's a good thing that job went to Zia Ariana. She is without a doubt 'to the throne bred.'"

Topher waved his hands away. "Nonsense," he said. "Your mother was just as qualified. Not the right birth order. And we all know about that."

"Toph, at least you'll never have to worry about the problem of having to run Monaforte," Pippa said. "I mean even Zander has a slight chance of it. Like, say, maybe if he pushed Adrian out a window or something."

They all laughed.

"Can you imagine? Last thing Zander would want is any responsibility," Topher said. "It's all he can do to manage himself. It's why I cut him such slack."

Pippa rolled her eyes. "Cut him slack? That's not what I heard after the wedding brunch."

Clementine interrupted. "Pippa—"

"I'm just saying I heard there was a confrontation."

"Look, Pippa, we both know that Zander loves to get a rise out of me. And you're fully aware of exactly how he does it."

Pippa and Clementine looked at each other and suppressed giggles until they could no longer hold it and burst out laughing.

"Sorry, Toph. You practically begged for that one," Sebastian said with a wink. "After all, we know the one most likely to get a rise out of you is you, not anyone else."

Topher looked at them all and shook his head. "I guess I deserved that one." He flipped the finger to his friend with a laugh. "But getting back to the subject at hand…" He paused, then hit his forehead with the heel of his hand. "Seriously, can I stop with the inadvertent metaphors already?"

"I'll drink to that," Pippa said, taking a large swig of her wine as Sebastian refilled everyone's glasses.

"Okay," Topher said. "Let's try this again. I know Zander has my back and that it's simply his childish way of staying relevant. And now I'd better keep my mouth shut, except for eating, before I put my foot in it ten more times."

As they ate, the foursome chatted about Monaforte and mutual friends and the various universities they attended. Just as they were finishing their meal, an oversized mango-orange moon arose and hovered over the tops of palm fronds that rustled in the wind along the nearby shore.

"Wow," Clementine said. "This place is amazing. I don't know how you two suffer through living on this boat. It must be a real struggle, what with all this beauty."

"Yeah, well, somebody's got to enjoy it. Speaking of amazing," Sebastian said. "I almost forgot that I promised to take you over to the Willy-T for a drink."

"The Willy-T?" Pippa said.

"It's a huge steel sailboat anchored not far from here in the Bight at Norman Island," Topher said. "Best known for people getting naked and jumping from the top deck or doing naked belly shots."

"Awesome! Let's go then," Pippa said. "Sounds like it'll be a great show."

Clementine got up from the table and motioned to Sebastian to hurry over to the dinghy.

Love Is in the Heir

"Sorry, Pips," she said. "But Sebastian promised to take only me. Sort of making a date of it."

She made an exaggerated wink to Sebastian, who returned a similar wink of collusion back at her.

Pippa gave her a hard stare. "You know you're about as subtle as a bitch in heat at a dog show."

Clementine just smiled.

"Fine, I can take the hint," Pippa said, holding her hands up. "Leave us here to clear the table."

"Perfect. Because I know you of all people can then find a more enterprising use for that tabletop," her friend said as she reached out for Sebastian's hand to lower herself into the dinghy.

Chapter Thirteen

WITHIN minutes, the two of them were motoring away without giving Pippa a chance to even object. Which left her and Topher staring at each other over the remains of their lobsters.

"Well," she said as she propped her elbows on the table and leaned her chin over her clasped hands.

"So," he said, pushing his plate out of the way.

"Um, yeah," she said, raising her eyebrows and flaring her nostrils, lips pursed.

"Yup," he added, drumming his fingers.

Silence pervaded for about forty seconds, which felt like an hour to Pippa.

"So, are you ready to talk about things yet?" Topher said.

"What things?" Pippa said, shifting her lips to one side and rolling her eyes upward, feigning ignorance.

"Like how you're conflating your anger at my brother with anger at me."

"I am not."

"Okay then. So why are you angry at me?"

Pippa paused for a minute, clearly unable to give a legitimate reason. She puffed her cheeks full of air and moved the air bubble back and forth between her cheeks. Then she cleared her throat to stall for some more time. "Oh, I dunno… Maybe because you conspired behind my back to get me here?"

Topher held up his hands in surrender. "I did no such

Love Is in the Heir

thing. All I said to Clem was that I'd owe her a lobster dinner if she managed the impossible."

Pippa's eyes grew large. "She sold me out for a damned lobster? Are you kidding me? What kind of friend is that?"

"The very best kind," he said with a smile, "who wants only the best for her good friend."

"And *you're* what's best?" She took another large swig of wine and stared at Topher, who was actually looking better and better to her as the evening progressed and she really started to let her guard down.

"Do I have to remind you?" he said as he stood up and reached for her hand, pulling her up. A soft, Brazilian jazz song was playing, one of those tunes written for pure seduction. Before Pippa could stop him, he enveloped her in his arms and began to slow dance with her, her head tucked beneath his chin, the two of them still in their swimsuits, which meant a lot of skin on skin and felt far more delicious to her than she'd remembered. He reached behind and pulled out the band that held her tight braid, running his fingers through her hair to loosen it up.

As she moved so slowly in Topher's arms, Pippa couldn't help but be reminded of dancing with him at Adrian's wedding, which quickly led to romancing, which ultimately led to all sorts of unnecessary drama, and she hated drama. But she didn't have it in her to fight him anymore. After all, he was a really nice guy. And the sex *was* pretty spectacular. And that thing of his was truly record setting in size. Besides, he felt so warm and hard and, well, hard. And growing harder by the minute, from the feel of things. The motion of the boat on the gentle swell of the harbor seemed to match perfectly the music and their own rhythm.

Jenny Gardiner

Soon she felt his fingers gently lift her chin, as his lips quietly touched her forehead, then the bridge of her nose, then the tip of it, finally finding her soft lips as he moved her chin just enough so he could reach her mouth.

Their breathing grew louder as the kiss intensified, his tongue entwined with hers as she softened into his grip, even pulling him toward her with her hands that had settled on his behind. She heaved a sigh, and she wasn't sure if it was one of abandonment or contentment. Either way, she knew she couldn't fight whatever it was that kept pulling the two of them together despite her strong will.

Topher's hands grazed her back and soon slipped beneath the edge of her bikini bottom where his warm hands settled on her behind, pulling her closer toward him as Pippa reached up to pull his head closer to hers.

They stood that way, hardly moving but for their mouths entwined, exploring one another with their tongues. He came up for air and pressed his forehead to hers.

"I think you know where I'm going with this," he said, breathing heavily. "But I really want to be respectful of your wishes, and I definitely don't want you to end up regretting anything we might do. So before we go any further, I need to be sure you're with me here."

Pippa paused, trying to figure out what it was that she wanted, knowing damn well she wanted him, there, now, even if that might not be the wisest move on her part.

"Are you looking for me to sign a consent form, then?" she asked, licking his lips, trying to get past the chitchat and back to the action.

Man, all it takes is a few glasses of wine to oil you up, girl, she thought. So much for your strong resolve that pursuing Topher was an overall bad idea.

Love Is in the Heir

"I'll settle for oral consent," he said, his hand reaching up to tug on the string of her bikini top.

"Oral sounds good to me," she said with a coy wink, knowing full well what she was telling him.

That was all the consent he needed, and with two short tugs he made quick work of her top, which sprang loose and tumbled to the ground. He leaned forward, weighing her breasts with his hands, alternating stroking each of her nipples with his tongue, a kid in a candy shop, indulging in as much as he could.

Reflected moonlight rippled in the soft swells of the water as Topher reveled in the soft swells in front of him, while Pippa leaned her head back, lost in the sensation his tongue bathing her nipples was sending deep within her.

Suddenly he stood up and grabbed her hand. "This is going to be so much better on the trampoline," he said, pulling her toward the bow of the catamaran.

Pippa pictured them having sex while jumping on a trampoline and started to laugh.

"That doesn't sound very romantic to me," she said.

"Just you wait," he said. "I think you'll be glad we made the move."

Once on the bouncy surface, he lowered himself onto the webbed netting, taking advantage of his angle to quickly shimmy her bikini bottom down as well, then pulling her toward his face and burying his tongue in her center.

"Oh, God. Baby, you're so wet," he said, groaning as he slipped a finger inside her.

Pippa let out a loud moan.

"Spread your legs more," he said, helping to shift her to straddle his face.

She was happy to cooperate if this was her reward. He pressed a hand against her behind, allowing him easier access as he stroked his tongue along her clit and moved first one then two fingers in and out of her.

The gentle lapping of water against the hull combined with the enthusiastic lapping of Topher's tongue against her wet center and the glide of his fingers were all Pippa could focus on as her breathing became heavy and her moans louder until finally she broke, shouting out his name as she came against his talented tongue and lips.

Topher wasted no time pulling his swim trunks off and Pippa on top of him, where she easily slid down over his erection and held still, pressed body to body, enjoying the sensation of being so filled up. Soon she began lifting her hips and pressing back down, joining him as he forged himself into her warmth, the two of them savoring the slide and release of their bodies. She leaned forward enough to allow his mouth to encircle her nipple, and she knew she wouldn't last long with his tongue working magic there while his cock filled her so deeply. He began to move faster, and with one last thrust, he came in her just as she let go, falling over the abyss along with him.

They lay there, still joined and in a relaxed state of near-perfect bliss as the sailboat bobbed on the water, her head pressed against his chest as he stroked her hair, their breathing in sync. Finally Topher rolled Pippa over till his face was inches from hers.

"There, now. That wasn't so bad, was it?" he said as he pressed his lips softly to hers. He kissed a trail to her chin, then along the column of her neck to that sensitive spot at the base of her throat.

"It was dangerously not so bad," she said, squirming suggestively beneath him, trying to stir him into action yet again. "So much so that if I'm not careful, I could become addicted to this."

"In that case give me a minute," he said. "I'm as ready as you are for round two. I only need to get my friend on board."

"I thought you finally got your friend on board," she said, aiming her thumb at herself.

"You mean you? Seriously? That was more like a miracle for the ages," he said. "I'm not even sure how it happened. Although I won't question it. But getting mini me ready for another go will take a moment more."

"I've got news for you, buddy. Mini me isn't so mini."

"You think so?"

"Trust me," she said. "He's your best spokesperson."

"Wouldn't that be spokes*penis*?"

They both laughed.

"Or maybe spokes*member*. Sounds more socially acceptable," Pippa said.

"So you're telling me if I had a small cock you'd not have come back for more?"

"You make me sound so shallow," she said. "But, uh, yeah." She smacked him playfully. "You know what they say? Go big or go home."

"Speaking of big," Topher said, looking downward. "A little more attention toward him and this project will be greenlighted in no time."

"In that case, lights, cameras, action," she said, scooting down his hard body, taking his not-so-mini me into her mouth.

Topher groaned. It was going to be a long night. In a very good way.

Chapter Fourteen

HOURS later, Topher stirred at the sound of a dinghy motoring toward them.

"Oh, crap," he muttered, leaning over to nudge Pippa.

"One little detail we forgot about when we fell asleep *al fresco*," he said in a whisper. "Sebastian and Clem returning."

Pippa sat up in a panic. "Christ, I'm naked!" she said. "Quick, what should we do?"

Topher pushed her down onto the trampoline again. "Keep low so they don't see you! I've got an idea."

He crawled along the webbing until he reached a hatch that opened to his cabin below. The window opening was wide enough for him to slip in head first until he was suspended, waist-deep.

"Careful! Don't want to get those dangly bits tangled up there," Pippa said.

"Trust me, that is of utmost concern to me right now."

He stretched his arms and fumbled in the dark room until he grabbed ahold of his blanket and tugged hard enough to pull it loose from the bed. It was only then he realized there was no way he was going to get back out the way he had come in as his arms couldn't provide the leverage needed to pull himself out. He shifted his hips, hoping to make enough space to perhaps slip one arm back up through the hatch so that maybe he could somehow pull the rest of his body out, but no go.

Love Is in the Heir

"What's wrong?" Pippa asked with a hiss. "The motor is nearby. They're going to be here any minute, and I'm haven't got a stitch of clothing on!"

"Um, this probably doesn't need to be stated, but I have my bare ass sticking up in the air straight in the direction they'll be walking any minute now. I'm well aware of our dilemma."

Pippa took one look at him and laughed. "Well, crap. What are we supposed to do?"

"I need you to go down below to my cabin so that you can push me up from there."

"I can't get down there without them seeing me!"

"Look at it this way," Topher said. "Either way they're going to see you. But at least this way you have control over which view they get."

Pippa thought about that for a moment. He had a point there.

"Fine," she said. "But I'm doing this under duress."

"Watch that you don't trip over the boom. It's dark out there."

She looked down at him, at least the half she could see, and her eyes grew large.

"Wait a minute," she said. "You are hanging upside down from a boat hatch, completely nude, with your white butt competing with the moon in its brilliance, and you're sporting a hard-on?"

Sure enough, he had an undeniable boner springing up.

"I can't help it," he said with a moan. "I started to think of you coming down to my cabin and that I'd be looking down at you while you're naked and pushing up on me with your tits bouncing around, and that's all it took."

"Men," Pippa said, rolling her eyes. "Sometimes your gender is so pathetic."

She started to slink low along the portside of the sailboat, hoping to stay down enough to avoid detection by the fast-approaching dinghy. But while she was busily focusing on the approaching boat, she failed to see what was right in front of her, and before she knew it, she stepped right into another hatch, this one leading to her own cabin.

"Sonofabitch," she shouted out loud.

"Shhhhh," Topher said. "Wait a minute. Are you okay?"

"Do you think I'd be okay if I shouted out obscenities?"

"What's wrong?"

"My foot slipped into my hatch." Pippa pulled her leg up to see a lovely gash bleeding from her shin. "I'm bleeding."

"Oh, Pips, quick, get the first aid kit," he said. "It's in the galley, the cabinet closest to the steps."

"I can't deal with treating this right now," she said. "I have to rescue you before they get back or we'll never live this one down."

"Great," Topher said. "Another laughable story about you and me, and me with a hard-on, no less. Thank goodness Zander's not here at least."

"Look, I'm on my way. Stay where you are."

"Pretty sure I'm not going anywhere in the foreseeable future."

"Good point."

Pippa hobbled toward the stern, cutting past the cockpit and the helm of the boat, which she grabbed on to

Love Is in the Heir

for support as she limped. She climbed down the steps, through the salon, over to Toph's cabin.

"It's dark in here," she said. "You're blocking the moonlight."

"Flip on the light," he said. "Just to your right."

She fumbled along the wall in the dark with her hands till she found the switch, finally illuminating the room. And what she saw, an upside-down, red-faced (not just from embarrassment) Topher, looked so damned hilarious she couldn't help but cackle out a laugh. Really loudly.

"Keep it down!" Topher said. "Now get over here. Climb on to the berth. I need you to grab my fists and straighten out your arms and push."

"Wait a second," Pippa said. "It looks like I do have to do something about this cut or I'll bleed all over your bed."

"I told you to treat it!"

"I don't have time to get it all fixed up. I'll grab some paper from the loo and stick it on there."

But when Pippa walked into the head to grab toilet paper, she realized she was trailing blood all over the white tiled floor.

"One minute," she said. "I've got to run some water on this thing or it's going to be a bloody mess. Literally."

"Hurry!"

The two of them were so engrossed in their goings-on they failed to notice that someone had boarded the vessel.

"Hurry for what, mate?" a voice shouted from the stern.

"Fuck!" Topher said.

But Pippa couldn't hear it, what with the water running in the head.

"Well, well, well. What have we here?" a voice right

above Topher said.

"Zander?" Topher said. "What in bloody hell are you doing here, Zander?"

"The better question is what the hell are you doing *there*?" his brother said. "Here I come to extend the olive branch to my kid brother for being such a prick, and I find you sticking out naked from the hatch with your own prick flapping around. What gives?"

"You okay?" Pippa shouted to Topher. "I'm almost done. This sucker doesn't want to stop bleeding."

"Bleeding?"

"Christ, Zander, stop with the questions and pull me out already."

"If you insist, but don't make me touch that thing of yours," he said. "I'm going to grab your ankles and pull on the count of three. One. Two. Three."

With that he pulled hard, and Topher's lower half finally slipped through the small opening, and he landed with a thud on the deck once his brother let go.

"What was that?" Pippa said, running into the cabin, only to peer up and see Zander, of all people, looking down into the hatch. She quickly crossed her left knee over her right leg and her arms over her chest, naively thinking that would provide enough modest protection, forgetting it was Zander there. Instead she just looked like she had to pee really badly.

"Good God, Pips, what the hell are you doing here? Like that?" Zander said. "And where are your clothes? And the blood—"

He looked at Topher, then at Pippa, who was reaching for the sheet since Topher had already managed to pull the blanket up with him, then glanced at Topher yet again.

Love Is in the Heir

"Okay. I get it," he said, starting to back away, rubbing his forehead with his hands.

"What're you doing here, Z?" his brother asked. "I don't recall sending out invites."

"Indeed," Zander said. "I was feeling badly about everything that happened, what with the thing with you and Pips and all."

With all the commotion, no one noticed Clem and Sebastian had returned.

"My God, it looks as if someone's been slaughtered here," Clementine said when she flicked on a nearby light, revealing a trail of blood leading down the steps. "What's with the carnage? Pips? Everybody okay?"

Clementine raced down the steps, following the trail of blood, to come upon her friend partially clad in only a white blood-stained sheet.

"What in bloody hell is going on here?" Clementine said just as she heard Sebastian burst out in laughter above them.

Clementine looked up to see Zander peering down at her.

"Well, this must be one hell of a story I can't wait to hear," Sebastian said.

"Shut up and don't laugh," Topher said.

"Um, I feel very much as if I'm not supposed to be witnessing something here. Only I don't know quite what it is," Clementine said. "But I'm worried about what is bleeding on you, Pippa. Can I help somehow?"

"Cripes, I thought I was going to lose the circulation to my lower half," Topher said above them.

"I'm pretty sure your lower half took a vote and wouldn't let that happen, judging by what I saw a few minutes ago," Pippa said.

"Ha, ha, very funny," Topher said.

"Anyone care to enlighten us about what happened?" Sebastian said.

Topher sighed. "It's a long story. Probably not really relevant to any of you."

Zander's eyes widened. "Are you joking? We're all standing around, and you haven't got any clothes on, and you're hanging ass over tea kettle from a boat hatch. If this isn't a story all of us need to hear, nothing is. In fact"—Zander pulled out his phone—"I need to record this for posterity."

Topher took one look at his brother trying to videotape him and flipped out, running after his brother.

"Toph! No! It's not worth it!" Pippa shouted from below before she turned to run upstairs to handle things on the same level.

But it was too late. Topher plowed into Zander, forcing him backward and over the railing into the dark waters below.

Chapter Fifteen

IF a feud had been simmering before, it had come to a full boil by dawn.

"What the hell is the matter with you?" Zander asked his bleary-eyed brother, who had been shooting him daggers with his eyes. Zander had changed out of his drenched clothes into a pair of swim trunks and a T-shirt from the small duffel he'd arrived with. Pippa had retreated to bed, humiliated, and Sebastian had already zonked out from too many drinks on the Willy-T, but the others were engaged in conversation still.

"How the hell did you even find me here?" Topher asked.

Clementine turned red and gulped, raising her hand. "I might be the guilty party there."

Topher knit his brows. "You told Zander we were coming here?"

"Oh, God no!" she said. "But I posted something on Facebook the other day on Topher's wall telling him that we were en route."

"Even if he saw that, how did my brother know where you were headed to?"

Zander tipped his pointer and middle finger from his forehead. "I am right here, you know," he said. "You don't have to talk as if I'm a nonentity here. And I'm not stupid. All I needed to do was get in touch with Mum's scheduling secretary to find out where you were."

Toph snapped his fingers in disappointment. "Damn.

Never thought Julia would betray me like that."

"It wasn't exactly a betrayal," his brother said. "I had an open invitation from Richard Branson to check out Necker Island nearby. I knew you'd been in the British Virgin Islands before and figured it was likely you'd come back here when you fled after the wedding. So I mentioned to Julia that I was thinking of a little trip to Necker, and she told me I should stop by to see you if I went there. Of course, I needed specifics about where you'd be. GPS is a godsend, by the way."

Topher grumbled. "Nothing like being practically off the grid to be readily available."

"Look, Toph, I came here to bury the hatchet," his brother said. "I didn't like how we'd left things, and I wanted to make it up to you."

"Looks like you did that in spades," Topher said. "Thanks a bunch for that."

"What do you mean thanks a bunch?" Zander was beginning to sound indignant.

"Look, Z, I finally started to right the ship as it were with Pippa, and then all of a sudden you show up at the perfectly wrong time. Plus I can't even begin to focus on things with her now that you're here. Throw in that whole fiasco last night," Topher said, "and all of you being privy to it, popping out one after the other like those miserable clowns in the little cars at the circus, and I can only imagine how that is going to be the next circle of hell of complete humiliation for me every time I'm around the family."

"Topher don't let that worry you," Clem said. "Pippa doesn't care."

Topher looked up from behind thick lashes, his gray eyes doubtful. "You're seriously going to tell me that,

Love Is in the Heir

Clem? After what it took to get her here after the last time?"

Clem sighed. "Okay, fine. Maybe you've got a point there. But let's not leap to conclusions. We can let Pippa speak for herself when she gets up."

"Look, I'm going out for a swim. I don't want to deal with this. You can laugh amongst yourselves at my expense. Have fun."

With that he got up, gathered his snorkeling gear, and jumped off the stern into the gentle blue Caribbean water.

Pippa awoke, sprawled atop her bed, staring out the porthole window and mulling over the events of the night before. She really didn't want to come out from the cabin until the coast was clear. But how could the coast ever be clear on a forty-foot-long catamaran unless everyone fell overboard and got eaten by sharks?

And what did a clear coast even mean to her? Who did she want gone from the boat? Surely she didn't want Topher to leave. Besides, it was his home for now, not hers. Plus she'd finally stopped being stupid about everything. Why would she change her mind now that she realized she really wanted to try this relationship on for size? Especially after such an amazing time of it last night. Well, for the first half of the night, at least. And she really had to give Zander credit for manning up and seeking out his brother to apologize to him. Although damn, could that timing have worked out any worse?

She tried hard to focus on her time with Topher from last night. And at first, that helped. After all, it was one hell of a night. First off, it was great to stop playing the stubborn stick-in-the-mud and finally yield to their mutual attraction. She knew that wasn't going to burn itself out anytime soon, and at some point she was going to have to ride that horse in the direction it was galloping.

But then just the whole experience. His warm skin pressed against hers while they danced as he sensually ran his fingers through her hair. His lips on hers, his tongue finding hers in its own frenzied dance. His fingers as they roamed across her body. His mouth as he brought her to climax with that skillful tongue of his. His most *un*-mini me, filling her up so perfectly; whether she was on top or beneath him or he behind her, it had been so right, all while rocking to the soothing swell of the Caribbean waters.

The more she dwelled on it, the more she knew she had to face everyone and get it over with. Then she and Topher could pick up right where they had left off. Well, maybe not quite there, with him dangling naked from the hatch and her bleeding like a beheaded chicken.

She looked down at the large Band-Aid secured to her shin and smiled at her small battle scar. Worth it if it meant she could have a few more command performances like last night before returning to Monaforte. The departure date for which she didn't even know yet. Come to think of it, lingering in this tropical paradise a little longer could be tempting… She wondered if Topher might be thinking just the same thing. She was sure Clementine wouldn't mind returning home without her. Maybe she'd feel like she'd succeeded with her trap, anyhow, and feel that much more proud of her skills as a matchmaker.

Whatever, Pippa wasn't going to worry about it. Instead, she'd talk to Topher right away and get it all

Love Is in the Heir

straightened out so they could get on with getting it on.

Chapter Sixteen

PIPPA finally drummed up the courage to face her friends, all of whom had seen her in some state of near nakedness only hours before or were at least clearly aware of what had gotten her to that condition last night.

She climbed down from her luxury berth, momentarily enjoying being sore in all sorts of places from their little foray on the boat's trampoline. Boy, who knew trampolines could be so much fun? She brushed her teeth and washed her face and even applied makeup and waterproof mascara to look her best while snorkeling. She rifled through her duffle for her tiniest bikini and while doing so came across the cache of condoms her friend had so blithely packed for her.

At first she was again annoyed that Clem would presume Pippa was going to welsh on her resolution to steer clear of Topher (even though she had done just that). But then she started to freak out a tiny bit because she realized that yet again, in their haste to consummate last night, not once did she think to even use the damned things.

Quickly, Pippa started to do the mental menstrual math to try to figure out if she was in the safe-zone. Amazingly, not even once had she considered the potential health hazards of going bareback, but she sure as hell didn't want to risk a pregnancy on top of all that. Sure, she'd been on the pill forever, but had she even remembered to take that thing yesterday morning? She was classic for forgetting

Love Is in the Heir

it. And that didn't matter so much when she wasn't sleeping with anyone, which she hadn't been in ages. Well, except for Topher at the wedding. It was easy to lapse under the circumstances. But then this. Argh. Such an inconvenience. Nevertheless she scrambled to find the packet and made sure she swallowed the thing ASAP.

She slipped a sun cover-up over her head, pressed it down so she looked straight and put together, and then climbed the stairs to the deck to greet her friends.

"Well, look who it is, all glowing and gorgeous this fine morning," Zander said with a wink.

"The glow could be from the wine," Pippa said, blushing.

"Or it could be because you were well and truly—"

"Don't say it, Clem," Pippa said with a warning tone in her voice. "Not gonna go there."

"What?" her friend said, acting all innocent. "I was just gonna say 'rhymes with luck.' After all, it took a bit of luck to get to that point."

Pippa rolled her eyes. "Please can we not delve into details here? Bad enough you were all witness to things, but I wouldn't mind preserving the sanctity of—"

Zander started to snicker, which got Sebastian to smile.

"Children," Pippa said lifting her hands in mock defeat. "What on earth has you behaving like ten-year-old boys now?"

"Sanc*tity*," Clementine said, shaking her head.

"What's so funny about *that* word?" Pippa said.

"Pips. Consider the source. Second half of the word," Clem said. "Something they saw on you last night, before you were properly draped."

Pippa pretend bashed her head into the nearest surface, a pole holding up the roof to the cockpit. "Why did I think we could all act like mature adults here?"

"Because you're female," her girlfriend said. "You're giving them too much credit if you think they're going to do anything other than *tit*ter—sorry—over what happened. You know and I know that what's done is done and you're moving on, but they just have to behave like schoolchildren for a while until they find a different distraction."

"Or get drunk," Sebastian added. "That usually works."

"In that case, let's break out the mimosas," Pippa said. "I'm starving and thirsty and could use a distraction from this nonsense."

Zander sidled up to her. "Work up an appetite last night, did you?"

"Seriously, Z. Do I give you the fifth degree each time you bang some pathetic royal-sniffing supermodel?"

"Uh, yeah," he said, laughing.

"Okay, so maybe I do give you a hard time about that. But you deserve it, because you're male-whoring around. There's a difference between spreading your seed, which is your habit, and having adult relations with someone."

Zander shook his head. "Right. So let me get this straight. For me it's a seedy—excuse the pun—one-night stand, but for you it's 'having relations'?"

Pippa looked at Clementine for support. "Help me out here, sister."

Clementine stood in front of Zander as if to make a

Love Is in the Heir

point.

"Chicks," she said, holding up her finger for her tutorial, "are classier. We don't go in for the sleaze thing you guys do. You only want to get your rocks off. We are looking for more connection than that."

Pippa had to momentarily block out images of her joy when Topher went down on her, thinking perhaps there was perhaps a hint of hypocrisy, because if she were truthful, it wasn't such a bad side benefit, getting those figurative rocks off.

Zander put his arm around Clem's shoulder. "Okay, now I get it. But just to clarify... Let's say you have a couple who are out partying, and things get a little out of hand, and while doing naked body shots maybe there's a little bit too much PDA that happens. Is that a special connection?"

Clementine blanched. "What did Sebastian say to you?"

Pippa's eyes grew wide, and she nodded at Clem. "You?" she mouthed to her friend.

Clementine scrubbed her hand over her face.

"I didn't say anything to anyone," Sebastian said, holding up his hand and X-ing his finger across his chest. "Promise and cross my heart."

"What are you talking about, Zander?" Pippa said.

"Let's say on my way here last night I made a little pit stop," he said. "I was thirsty after a long flight, and the place came highly recommended."

"Oh my God," Clementine said.

"What happens at the Willy-T stays at the Willy-T, folks," Sebastian said. "That's the number one rule of the place."

Jenny Gardiner

Clementine knit her brows and mouthed, "Really?" so that only he could see. He winked at her to reassure her.

"I'm not saying I saw anything," Zander said. "I'm merely saying it looked as if some people were having a *really* good time. Like there was quite a special connection." He made finger quotes to emphasize her terminology.

"Seriously, Clem? Naked body shots?" Pippa whispered to her friend.

"Stop," she said. "At least I wasn't nude and bleeding with a guy suspended from the ceiling."

Pippa elbowed her in the ribs.

"Okay, so it looks as if the only one who comes out smelling clean after last night is Zander. But that's only because he's got a ring in his nose now, thanks to Andi," Pippa said. "Nevertheless, I've got enough dirt on him to shut him up for a while, at any rate."

"We all agree that none of this ever happened then?" Clementine said.

Zander hung his head.

"Aw, man," he said. "I was just getting going. This was going to be my entertainment for the day."

"No more talk or everyone will find out the true story behind you and Andi," she said. "Besides, you owe it to me for my interventions on your behalf with her."

Pippa looked around, finally noticing a missing person.

"Where's Topher?" she said. "Did he go back to sleep?"

Sebastian shrugged. "He was irritated earlier. Finally got up and collected his snorkeling gear and dove in."

"How long ago was that?"

The three of them looked at each other, and Sebastian shrugged, thrusting out his lower lip. "Maybe an hour? I

Love Is in the Heir

seem to have lost track of time what with all this intimate talk." He gave Pippa a joking shove on the shoulder.

"I'm going in after him," she said, pulling off her cover-up, which led to some catcalls from Zander.

"Pippa's the man with the plan," he said, clapping and whistling.

"Look, Pips," Clem said. "Maybe give Toph a chance to breathe. He was stressed out. I'm sure it's good for him to blow off some steam in the water. He'll come back, and all will be fine."

She pulled out a bottle of champagne from the fridge.

"In the meantime, mimosas, anyone?"

Chapter Seventeen

TOPHER loved the ocean. So much so that it felt like an extension of his very being. And if he had to get away and escape his worries, there was no better place for him to do so than submerged in pristine azure waters, taking in the extraordinary scenery, feeling almost a part of that underwater world. Somehow clarity prevailed for him under the sea.

And today, he sure needed some clarity.

As he wove between reefs and along rock outcroppings, he thought about all that had happened. He couldn't help but dwell on just about everything to do with Pippa, but especially last night. At the time, he was afraid he'd completely drop the ball, he was so excited to finally get Pippa right where he wanted her. That would've been all he'd needed: to finish before he started. But once he finally persuaded her to join in the fun, man, did they have a good time of it. Just imagining her standing in front of him once that bikini top dropped, he thought he'd lose it right then and there all over again. Is that possible in the ocean? Or are there laws of physics that would prevent that? He was glad the seagoing creatures wouldn't notice the burgeoning bulge in his swim trunks.

Despite his obvious horniness at the mere thought of Pippa, he knew he had to approach this situation with a clear head. And while they had chemistry to spare, things clearly weren't clicking the way they needed to. Each time they were together, something disastrous happened, which

Love Is in the Heir

inevitably involved his family, precisely the thing he was trying to avoid by being an ocean away from them. So if bringing Pippa into his world was going to invite all that other nonsense in, then logic would hold that she and Topher weren't going to work out.

He knew she'd be so upset about this, especially since she'd only finally come around herself. But upon further reflection, Topher was finally recognizing that Pippa had been right all along in trying to nip this thing in the bud. It was sheer folly to have these heated and passionate couplings and then have to deal with the backlash that resulted from them. *Hanging from the hatch… Seriously, who needed that grief?* As soon as he got back to the boat, he'd break the news to her.

Too bad it didn't seem like the right time to break it to her.

"You ready to pull up anchor and head over to Peter Island?" Sebastian said when he climbed aboard the sailboat.

"Huh?"

"I thought it would be nice to go over to the resort. Maybe we'll swim with some sea turtles. We can grab lunch, and the ladies can see if there's space available at the spa," Sebastian said. "After all, we need to show them the best the BVI has to offer."

"What about my brother?" Toph asked. "Is he part of the crew now?"

"You don't want to get rid of me, do you?" Zander said.

Jenny Gardiner

"What do you think?" Toph said.

"Ouch," his brother said. "In that case, you're in luck. Branson's got a sailboat coming for me. We'll meet at Peter Island later today."

Topher would be happy to get rid of Zander. He loved his brother, but he was going to be waiting all day with bated breath for the teasing to begin. And the last thing he needed in his tropical paradise was to have Zander taint it with all that mockery he so remembered from his growing-up years. Funny how you can love your family but hate to be near them sometimes. In the meantime, he was going to be preoccupied with getting the boat under sail, so at least he'd have some distractions.

Sebastian began barking orders to everyone so that they could get going as soon as possible.

"Pippa, be sure any towels, bathing suits, or wet clothing hanging on the lifelines on the side of the boat are secured so they don't blow away. Clementine, close up cabinets below deck and make certain all dishes are put away so we don't have things flying everywhere below deck."

Zander was tasked with helping to weigh anchor without incident while Topher took care of checking the lines and hoisting the sails and Sebastian remained at the helm.

The cat was soon under sail, and Topher remained busy with the mainsheet and shouting orders to the others to work the jib sheet and mainsail whenever the boat tacked. All of which gave Topher a grace period in which he didn't need to lower the Pippa boom quite yet.

They arrived at Peter Island and dropped anchor in Dead Man's Bay near a stunning 130-foot yacht in royal

Love Is in the Heir

blue with gold tooling.

"And here I thought this is what you'd be out sailing on," Pippa said to Topher. "Little did I know you'd opt for the tiny little toy boat by comparison."

"Sure, I could do it in style if I wanted to mooch the royal yacht, but the whole idea is I'm out here on my own," he said. "No handouts from the family, and better still, no grief from them either." He gave a nod toward his brother, who was helping to be sure the anchor had indeed anchored.

"But we're past that now, right?" Pippa said, reaching for his hand. Topher was being elusive, however, and the more she fished for mindless chitchat to assure her all was okay, the more he bristled at having to make conversation under the circumstances.

"Let's talk later," he said. "I've got a lot to do right now."

He set about tying up the sails once they were lowered and making sure the rigging and ropes were secured.

Once the sailboat was taken care of, Topher slathered on some more sunscreen and gathered up his snorkeling gear.

"I'm going in if anyone wants to join me," he said, although he'd have been happy to have the water to himself.

Pippa donned her mask, snorkel, and flippers and followed him in. The water was about twenty feet deep but clear enough to see grasses shifting with the water flow along the sandy bottom. Occasionally a fish or two would swim by, but it wasn't quite like swimming around the reefs, where there was always something happening somewhere if you watched closely.

But then a beautiful turtle drifted by, its flipper feet stroking through the water. Its cheery-looking head poked through the opening in the beautiful amber scalloped carapace.

Pippa came up for air and started yelling for the rest of the group to get in the water to see the turtle. Finally she and Topher went beneath the surface where several more turtles were milling about, swimming slowly toward their unknown destination.

She tapped Topher on the back, motioning for him to see the turtles. But he didn't need to have them pointed out to him. Sea turtles had become his Zen, and he could commune with them underwater for hours, at peace with the world. The minute he spotted them, his breathing and heart rate settled down significantly.

The two of them remained suspended in the water, barely moving but to keep up with the tortoises. It could have been a magical moment if Topher wasn't focused on what he had to do.

After about thirty minutes, the turtles had scattered and were no longer near enough to watch. Pippa surfaced and removed her mask just as Topher did.

"Oh, my God! That was incredible," she said with a squeal. "I can't believe we hung out in the water with them with their cute little turtle flippers and those little tails and their faces! They look like old men! I felt like a turtle whisperer. I think they liked me! What do you think?"

Topher grinned. "I'm sure they loved you, Pips," he said. "I mean, what's not to love." Even though he was going to have to focus on that very thing if he was going to shake her from his life as planned.

She wrapped her arms around his neck and squeezed

Love Is in the Heir

hard. Which was pure torture for poor Toph, feeling her body in that tiny bikini pressed up against him like that. And naturally his body was going to betray him by being involuntarily most receptive to her nearness. No way would Pippa not notice the rise in his swim trunks.

He knew he had to totally sever the cord before he succumbed to ill-advised temptation.

"Hey, Pips, let's go grab lunch on shore," he said. "There's a nice restaurant on the beach here. We can order some painkillers and enjoy some fresh fish. Sound good?"

She squinted her eyes at him. He knew his tone of voice didn't evoke much warmth. And he was sure she was wise to his not acting on her proximity and at least giving her a kiss. *It is time to cut the cord*, he repeated to himself. And no better place than in front of a restaurant full of people to avoid a scene.

Chapter Eighteen

"**HAVE** you noticed Topher acting distant all day?" Pippa said to Clementine as she dried off and grabbed a sarong from her duffle in her cabin.

Her friend shrugged. "He's probably a little distracted," she said. "It's a lot of responsibility to sail a boat, especially with guests on it. Plus he's probably super tired."

"Huh," she said. "I suppose that's possible."

Only she knew from past relationships that even if a guy was exhausted, he'd snap at the chance for physical interaction, especially in the early days of a romance. And no question about it, Topher didn't reciprocate one bit when she wrapped her arms around him. Sure she felt that hard-on creeping up, but hell, most guys could get an erection watching a commercial for underarm deodorant, so that meant nothing. If anything, his body betraying him like that and him showing no signs whatsoever of participation was not a good sign. She did not feel like she was in the driver's seat, and it didn't thrill her.

"It was a weird night," Clem said. "Give him a chance. I'm sure everything's fine. I mean look, we are in one of the most beautiful parts of the world. It's practically a recipe for romance. I'm sure once Topher gets some food in him and a drink to loosen him up, he'll be great."

Since when did a guy need a drink to get horny? Pippa wondered. But she kept quiet, hoping for the best.

Topher was waiting in the dinghy to motor to shore.

Love Is in the Heir

The others had decided to give the couple some space so stayed back on the boat to eat sandwiches and nap. Once they got to the sand, they beached the dinghy off to the side far from sunbathers and walked a hundred yards past guests lazily swinging in hammocks and others tooling around with tiny Sunfish sailboats. Still others were sound asleep on lounge chairs, books pressed to their chest. It was a quiet resort where you could be amongst plenty of people but still feel secluded.

The beach bar was tucked away just off the stretch of sugar sand, separated by discreet bushes but with a great view of the ocean. The hostess led them to a private table tucked away from others who were dining.

"Nice and private," Pippa said. "I like it."

Soon a waitress took their orders and delivered the promised Painkiller tiki drinks, which Pippa was about to need more than she even knew.

"Look, Toph," Pippa said. "I know things went a little haywire last night—"

"Haywire," he said, pausing. "Yes. That is quite true."

"But I hope that didn't scare you off," she said. "You've seemed a bit, well, tense today. And I'm hoping it's not that you've gotten cold feet or anything. Or that maybe I wasn't good or something?"

Topher shook his head, waving his hand. "Oh, gosh, no. You were perfectly fine," he said.

"Perfectly fine?" she said. "That seems like the way you'd describe a meal you ate at a fast food restaurant, not sex with someone who thought the sex was extraordinary."

Topher started stammering and blinking as if that could erase what he'd said and start again. "I didn't mean it wasn't great. I mean, it was fantastic. Really, it was."

Jenny Gardiner

"But—"

"Yes, but," he said with a sigh.

"There's always a but, isn't there?"

He shook his head. "I'm afraid there is, Pippa. You see, I'm like those little turtles who take off for the big bad world and leave their family behind," he said. "I'm off in the world, on my own. And I think I'm much better off not having to deal with all that family baggage. It only gets in the way of my life, Pippa. I'm better off drifting alone. I'm sorry."

"Yeah, but I'm not family baggage," she said, scrunching her brows as the waitress delivered her tuna steak. "I'm not even family. And I'd like to think I'm not baggage. But to tell you the truth, if you think I am, well, that's not exactly the most flattering description I've ever had attributed to me."

"No, no, no. I don't mean you're baggage," he said, averting her gaze, digging into his mahi as if his life depended on it. "I mean all the family stuff. I'm totally over it. I don't want it to cast a shadow on my adult life. And I'm afraid that there's a danger of that happening forever if you and I continue down the path we've started on."

Pippa squinted at him. "You're serious? We had the best night imaginable last night—well, until it became the worst night imaginable, but even that you kind of have to laugh at. Instead once again you're choosing to let your past define you. I don't get it."

Topher gave a feeble nod, chowing down on his fish with a ferocity it didn't deserve.

"You hungry?" she said. "Because you look like you're substituting inhaling that fish for having sex with me, you're so fervent with it."

Love Is in the Heir

He put his fork down. "Look, Pippa. I'm sorry. I'm not good at this stuff. I don't know what else to say. We had a lot of fun. But it's simply not gonna work out. It's not you. It's me."

Pippa was pissed. He took her to this romantic little beach bar to blow her off? Seriously? Why couldn't he have been man enough to just dump her while they were on the boat at least? So that she could then dump him right off the side of the thing.

"You know what, Topher?" she said, taking a deep breath. "You suck. You're being a coward and a complete child, worrying about what your brothers might say or do. But hey, that's okay. I'd rather know now that you can't handle it, so I guess I should thank you for showing me your true colors before I got in too deep. It's been real, but I have to go."

With that, she got up from the table and stormed away toward the beach. She didn't even wait for him to take her back to the boat by dinghy. Rather, she simply walked into that calm, clear-teal, turtle-loving water until she had no choice but to swim and freestyled her way back to the boat. The last thing Pippa Grimaldi would ever do was stick around where she wasn't wanted. She'd had enough experience being unwanted in a house with parents who had far more important things to deal with than her.

Chapter Nineteen

THE others were nowhere to be found when she boarded the vessel. She called out their names to no reply. But when she started walking down the steps, she heard the unmistakable sound of two people going at it coming from her friend's cabin.

"Et tu, Clementine?" Pippa muttered. "I can't even escape this place with a hint of dignity now, dammit."

She had no idea where Zander was hidden away but took a chance he was in Topher's berth and knocked hard, practically expecting to find him just as she'd found Topher all those years ago. It would, after all, only be fitting. But if it happened, she'd probably clobber the man.

"Enter!" Zander said.

She found him curled up on the bed with a copy of *Fifty Shades of Grey*.

"Honestly, the world is coming to an end," she said, shaking her head. "First your brother loses his shit, and now you're reading this two-bit, purple-prosed porn? What has gotten into you people? Show some respect, man!"

"Now, now," he said. "What makes you think I'm enjoying it?"

"That creepy grin on your face, maybe."

"I was curious to see what all the hoopla was about. Picked it up at the airport to read on the plane. It's kind of stupid, actually. Andi thought it was hilarious that I was reading it."

"Please, promise me you aren't going to impose icky

Love Is in the Heir

bondage things on her now," Pippa said. "Or maybe you already have. I mean who knows? I thought I knew you, but you're being so strange, and your brother's even worse. I totally need to get out of here. Take me with you. But first, I really need a drink."

"Aww, Pips. Don't tell me Toph petered out on you?" he said. "Forgive the pun."

"Yeah, his peter is out. Officially so. But frankly, he can have his damned peter. I don't need the thing. Though it sure did stand out in a crowd."

Zander burst out laughing. "Is this an ode to Topher's dick you're reciting right now? Should I turn on my phone and record this for posterity?"

"Do so and I'll kill you," she said. "I'm serious, Zander. I'm coming with you when that sailboat arrives. I have to get out of here and fast."

Zander stuck out his lower lip as he mulled the proposition over. "I don't see why not," he said. "I was really only planning to spend time at his resort just to find an excuse to come to the BVI to make up with Toph. I've done that now. And I couldn't bring Andi along, since that would have been awkward, so I have no one to hang out with."

"Well, since you can't have your new BFF along, I hope you can settle for your old best friend instead, Z," she said. "And I know you'll find the right thing to say to me so that I don't spend the next few days crying."

Zander reached out his arm to her as he patted the spot next to him on the bed. "Nah," he said. "You two weren't a thing long enough for you to be upset, Pips. Besides, he's a guy. Who gets upset over a guy anyhow?"

He gave her a wink, and she smiled weakly through a

thin haze of tears that made her hazel eyes bright with sadness.

♛

For the next hour or so until the sailboat arrived, Topher kept his distance from Pippa, tinkering with boat-maintenance issues. Cowardly, maybe. But it was all he could figure to do. He was a complete failure at being a sucky ex, if that's what he was now to Pippa. Not that they ever officially got to something official anyhow, but still. It was headed that direction.

But he knew it was best this way. Rip the Band-Aid off quickly and then let it heal. Sure, it hurt at first, but this way he could keep his distance from everyone and not deal with all the stuff that just stressed him out so much with family and relationships. He was better off being a free spirit, wandering on his own, the only anchor the one that secured the boat in place at night.

♛

Pippa threw all her belongings into a bag, even the still-damp sarong and bikini. She'd braided her hair back again in a long plait and donned yoga pants and a workout top. Carefree Pippa was gone, and real-world Pippa was back. She wanted to get out with her dignity somewhat intact as soon as she could at this point.

She was climbing the stairs when Clementine opened the door to her cabin. Clem was holding a sheet up to herself, her shoulders bare.

"Hey," she said to her friend. "What're you doing?"

Love Is in the Heir

"What does it look like I'm doing?"

"Um, taking your clothes to the cleaners, and you don't have a laundry bag?"

"Yeah. That," Pippa said. "Actually, I'm going with Zander as soon as his ride shows up."

"But what about you and Toph?"

Pippa drew her finger across her throat like a knife. "There is no me and Toph."

"Pippa, be real. Don't give up on him again. He's invested in you at this point. If you leave now, there's no turning back."

Pippa rolled her eyes. "I'm not giving up on anyone, Clem. He's the one bailing."

"Topher? Ditched you?"

Pippa shook her head. "Dropped me like a hot potato. I didn't even have a chance to defend myself. It was sort of weird."

Clementine pinched the bridge of her nose with her fingers. "Seriously I don't even know why I try," she said. "All this effort, and what has it gotten me?"

"I'd say it's gotten you a whole lot of naked belly shots with a near stranger, for starters," she said. "And now, from the sounds of it, a vacation quickie with the man as well."

"Quickie?" she said. "Why that wasn't quick in the least!" She put her hand over her mouth realizing her insensitive gaffe. "I'm sorry, Pips. That was inappropriate to rub that in under the circumstances."

Pippa waved her hand at her. "Whatever, hon," she said. "If you're happy, I'm happy. Although I'm not really happy, because Topher's an idiot. But that has nothing to do with you. Oh, and here—"

She rifled around in her bag, finally pulling out a handful of condoms and tossing them to Clem, who nearly dropped her sheet while trying to catch them.

"Here, at least they'll find a use with you."

"Well, at least you made a little dent in them," her friend said.

But Pippa shook her head no.

"You mean you never consummated the deal?" Clementine's eyes grew large with incredulity.

Pippa just looked at the ground.

"Oh, wow. You forgot them?"

Pippa nodded her head sheepishly.

"Pips! How could you? That's the most un-Pippa-like thing I think you've ever done!"

She shook her head. "I don't know. I don't know. *I don't know*," she said. "I guess we simply forgot. Or we didn't even think of it. I mean, we were kind of busy."

"What're you gonna do?"

"I'm going to leave here and never think about Topher again," Pippa said. "And if I see him at Zander's wedding, I'll politely nod my head and turn the other direction. And definitely not sleep with the next damned brother in that household."

Clem laughed. "You'd practically be assaulting a minor if you went after Luca."

"Not gonna happen," her friend said.

"But what if, you know?" Clementine rubbed her belly suggestively.

"Are you kidding? Uh, uh. Not gonna happen. Not on my watch."

"Hate to tell you, you might not have any control over that one, my dear."

Love Is in the Heir

"Well, we'll cross that bridge. In the meantime, I'm not going to worry about it."

Just then Topher yelled down to his brother.

"Uh, better get up here, Z," he said. "Your carriage awaits you."

Pippa gave Clem a hug. "You're welcome to join us, you know."

"Thanks," she said. "But I think I'll stick around here to see where things go. Maybe I can work on Topher for you."

"Nah. Don't bother," Pippa said. "Not gonna risk heartbreak with that one. He's too fickle to deal with. You gonna be okay here?"

"Definitely," she said, giving her friend a squeeze. "And you don't need me for moral support?"

"I'm good, Clem. Thanks for trying to matchmake us. I know your heart was in the right place, even if you were deceptive." She winked at her.

"I'm impressed you can even attempt to smile under the circumstances."

"Yeah, well, I'm not gonna let him see that it's affected me. Going out with my head held high."

♛

Topher stood on the bridge, motioning to the skipper of the dinghy coming to retrieve his brother.

He looked surprised to see Pippa coming ahead of Zander with her duffel bag.

"You're leaving?" he said.

"Uh, yeah," she said. "I've got no reason to stick around here. Zander and I are going to take a few days to play."

"You sure you don't want to hang out here?"

Pippa laughed a laugh with no humor behind it. "Thanks. I'll take a pass."

"Well, okay then," Topher said, extending his arm and grabbing her hand to shake it. "Take care of yourself."

Pippa stared at him, bug-eyed. "You're really going to shake my hand like we're finalizing some sort of business deal? After you spent half the night inside me barely twelve hours ago? Wow."

She turned and walked toward the skipper, who held her hand as she boarded the dinghy for the short ride to the opulent sailboat awaiting them. She never turned back even once.

"Good afternoon, Your Highness," the skipper said to Zander as he boarded the dinghy. "Sir Richard sends his kindest regards and offers with his compliments full use of the Necker Belle for the week."

Pippa looked up, and not a hundred yards away from them was the most magnificent catamaran she'd seen yet, over a hundred feet long, sleek, elegant, and just what the doctor ordered.

Now *this* was her favorite way to lick her wounds.

Chapter Twenty

PIPPA and Zander sat with their feet dangling over the edge of the boat. They'd finished a gourmet dinner of chateaubriand and topped it off with a flight of world-class wines. Here she was on a breathtakingly beautiful sailboat, guest of a man famed the world over for being a considerate host, alongside the man who had been her best friend since her mother pawned her off on Zander's governess when they were three years old. She should have been the happiest woman on the planet.

Yet not only was she not with Topher, who had managed to crawl his way into the deep recesses of her heart, she was never going to be with Topher, which was particularly wrenching after she'd finally capitulated, against her own better judgment, to let the man sneak into that fortress of a heart of hers.

She wasn't merely upset, she was ticked off.

"I don't get it, Zander," she said. "I mean what is wrong with that idiot brother of yours?"

She knew she was beginning to sound like One-Hit Hannah, repeating herself ad nauseam. No one wanted to hear someone moan and complain about a jilted lover, but that didn't prevent her from saying the same thing twenty different ways to Zander. She knew he'd understand though. That's what best friends were for.

Besides, in a way, she'd not even be dealing with this whole problem if it weren't for Zander. After all, she knew Toph because of Z. Plus Zander was the one who gave

Topher such abuse about the Episode, which led to the fallout after Adrian's wedding. Perhaps things would be entirely different had that not been the case. So the least he could do was listen to her complain for a while.

"Here Pips, have another drink," he said, pouring her another glass of wine.

"Promise you'll make sure I don't slump my way overboard?"

He laughed. "It's a deal."

Pippa suppressed a little sniffle. "I'd really started to care for him, Z," she said, only to start crying all over again. Poor Zander had been stuck trying to settle her down since they got on the boat.

"Look at this way," he said. "You don't like to be tied down, right? You travel all over the world for work. If you're stuck with one guy, then that's going to make it so much harder going away all the time. Think how sad that would make you. This way, you don't have to be sad about that!"

She thought about that for a second. "That is the most convoluted reasoning I think I've ever heard," she said. "Basically you're telling me, you're better off being sad now because if you were happy now, then you'd be sad later."

Zander shrugged. "Logic worked for me."

"The thing is, Zander, you know how much I suck at relationships. Remember that guy. What was his name?"

"See, you can't even remember the guy's name. You're not ready for a real relationship until you can commit their names to memory."

"Topher."

"Huh?"

"Topher. There. I said it. Topher. I've committed it to

Love Is in the Heir

memory."

"You're making this hard on me, Pips."

"I need to be serious now," she said. "I've been trying to understand why I'm not relationship material. And you know I'm not. I can't even find a date most of the time, let alone someone who wants to be around me for more than a night or two."

"I like to be around you all the time, Pips."

"That doesn't count," she said. "You're like my default brother, so you have to like to be around me."

Zander shook his head. "I don't know about that. My brother Topher doesn't like to be around me!"

"That's because you tease him mercilessly. If you would stop doing that, I can promise you he'd be your bestie."

"Guys don't have besties."

"Okay, well, enough about you. Let's get back to me. So I figured out my issues have to do with not knowing what a healthy relationship looks like. I mean look at my parents. They were so fly-by-night, I feel like they're almost strangers to me. I mean they stuck me in boarding school just so they didn't have to have me around."

"If it's any consolation, I went to boarding school."

"Yes, but that's different," she said. "That was part of your training to be royalty."

"Wouldn't it have made more sense to train someone to be royal by having them live with the people who are royal? In the royal palace?"

"So maybe, yeah, but you can't tell me your parents don't adore all of you," she said. "And simply the fact that there are so many of you, clearly they relished having a family."

Jenny Gardiner

"Okay, so you recognize that this is where you need to work on things, P. You want to be better at lasting relationships. I'd say that's great progress. You wanna go for a swim?"

She pointed to the water, illuminated from below by lights beneath the boat so that it looked like some vehicle from outer space. "Down there? With the waters probably teeming with sharks at night?"

"The water is lit up all around us, and it's perfectly clear," he said. "I think we'd see a shark long before he saw us."

"I'd rather drink my sorrows away."

"Fine, but can't say I didn't warn you when you have a bitch of a hangover tomorrow."

"Yeah, yeah," she said, topping off her wineglass. "You don't feel badly for me that I grew up as some latchkey child, a waif, unwanted, unloved?"

Zander scruffed her head. "Hate to tell you, Pippa, but waifs don't live in palatial cliffside estates with dramatic views of the Mediterranean," he said. "I think someone's having a self-indulgent pity party right now, so I'll not dignify that nonsense with a reply. You know your parents loved you in their own absentee way. And besides, you know my parents loved you to death too. So it's as if you've got two sets of parents. An added bonus. Lucky you!"

"Yeah, but I've always been this drifter girl, wandering around, floating in and out between circles of friends, never committing to a guy. And finally I commit to one, and instead he pulls away from me."

"Pips, that's called life. You win some, you lose some. And it all comes out in the wash."

"Wash," she said. "That reminds me, I need to do

Love Is in the Heir

laundry. You think they have a washing machine on this thing? I can't even find a washing machine that loves me."

With that Zander gave up on trying to reason with her. "Pips, my dear. Come along. I'm tucking you into bed. You win. I quit. Yes, the washing machine is not interested in a long-term relationship right now. Let's get you off to bed so you can prepare yourself for that massive hangover we talked about."

"Do you love me, Zander?" she said, still dressed in her yoga pants and top as he pulled the covers over her.

"You know I do, Pips. You're my bestie."

"I thought you said men don't have besties."

"Tell you what. You keep this one to yourself, and we can be besties forever."

"You promise?"

"Good night, Pippa."

Chapter Twenty-One

IF Topher could have smoke coming out of his nose, he would. As it was, he was like a fire-breathing dragon.

After he got frustrated while cutting into his steak at dinner and threw his fork and knife down, Sebastian read him the riot act.

"Dude," he said. "Chill out, man. I think you need to get laid. Or something to reduce the tension that's bouncing off of you."

"I don't want to talk about it."

"Fine, but don't spread your bad mood to us. Why don't you go back over to the Willy-T's," he said. "I'm sure you can find some topless babe to distract you."

Topher looked at him and glared.

"Look, Topher, let's talk about it," Clementine said. "You gotta admit you went from smoking hot to ice cold on poor Pippa back there. I'd imagine you must be pretty confused if you were willing to flip on her like that."

Topher then set his jaw and remained silent.

"Does it help if I tell you I understand where you're coming from?" Clementine said.

"Look, Clem, I don't really need you playing armchair shrink with me, okay?" he said. "It was fun until it wasn't fun, and then that reminded me that I was getting in too deep anyhow. I don't need to have an anchor around my neck right now."

"And Pippa's an anchor?" she said.

"All women are anchors," Sebastian said.

Love Is in the Heir

"Excuse me?" Clementine's voice raised an octave.

"Topher and I don't need to be tied down," he said. "We like to weigh anchor and go where the tide takes us sometimes. And you can't do that if you have a woman trying to pin you down."

"Trying to pin you down? What, like you're trapped like some sad butterfly being secured against a page of black velvet in somebody's butterfly collection?" she said. "*Pin you down.* As if."

"You know what I mean, Clem," he said. "I mean it's fine to hook up and all, but who needs all that long-term commitment nonsense."

"Right. I got it. Hookups, fine. Settle downs, not."

"Precisely," he said.

"Look, Clem, I'm not getting involved in this conversation because it can only devolve from here," Topher said. "And I don't want to say I'm never going to commit to a relationship. But right now, that idea is scary and uncomfortable to me, and I can't deal with it."

"Okay, so now we're getting somewhere," she said. "Scary and uncomfortable I can work with. Hookup Harry, not so much." She threw the stink eye at Sebastian, who was oblivious to her anger and cutting into his steak, happily taking a large bite.

"Tell me what has you so scared."

Zander shrugged. "I don't know, Clementine. I just don't feel comfortable with it."

"Is it because you feel too exposed, like you opened yourself up too much to her?" she said. "Or is it because you were too exposed to us?" She laughed. "Sorry, I couldn't help myself."

"Great. I finally spill my guts and you mock me," he

said. "This is precisely why I want nothing to do with any of it."

"I'm sorry you feel that way, Christopher," Clem said, invoking his full name, which his mother had only used on him when he was in trouble or in danger as a child. "Because sometimes in life you're going to have to be scared and uncomfortable. Sometimes you have to push through it and get out of your comfort zone and make room for a little growing up. I'm sorry that I went to all the trouble to bring Pippa here only for you to chicken out like you did and send her packing. But I'm almost even more sorry that I wasted my time 'hooking up' with the likes of Sebastian, who is clearly a selfish git who's doomed to grow old and alone someday and it'll serve him right."

With that, she got up and stormed off to her cabin, leaving the guys to look at each other and shrug before finishing up their meal.

"Toph?" Sebastian said after they'd finished cleaning up from supper.

"Yup?"

"You want to smoke some weed?"

Topher looked at him. "Are you serious?"

Sebastian nodded. "Got it from some guy I know in Road Town. Was holding on to it for just such an occasion."

"You mean when we've got a couple of chicks pissed at us?"

"Nah. I'm used to that. I was thinking sometime when there's no chance we can find anyone to hook up with in

Love Is in the Heir

the next two hours."

"Sometimes you gotta do what you gotta do, man," Topher said.

An hour later, the two men were sprawled out on the trampoline, staring up at the stars.

"That is so cool," Sebastian said.

"What?"

"That cluster of stars," he said, pointing off to the east.

"What's so great about them?"

"Reminds me of what you must've looked like with your bottom half sticking out of the hatch." He laughed out loud.

"A bunch of stars a billion light years away reminds you of my naked ass?"

"I don't know, man. I'm wasted. It just sounded good."

Topher lay there in practically the same spot he'd lain the night before, when Pippa had finally settled herself over his hard cock. It made him want a bag a chips. Or maybe it was the weed doing that.

"Shit, Sebastian," he said. "This wasn't such a good idea after all."

"Why not?"

"'Cause it should have taken my mind off of everything, but now I'm lying here thinking about having sex with a bag of chips."

"You're an idiot, Toph."

"But you love me, man."

"But not for hookups. Just remember that."

Which Topher didn't even hear, because he'd passed out and within minutes was snoring away, momentarily at peace with the world.

Chapter Twenty-Two

THE two men woke early with the sound of a dinghy approaching. For a fleeting second, Topher hoped it was Pippa. Maybe he could make amends to her.

He realized immediately it was no such thing, but rather it was Clementine's ride. She'd texted to shore to have a water taxi come for her first thing.

"It's been real, guys," she said. "But I'm outta here. One hookup too many for my liking."

Sebastian, still not getting it, reached over to give Clem a kiss, which she deflected by turning her face away and instead feeding him the back of her head and a chunk of her blond hair.

"See ya, Toph," Clem said, giving him a hug. Sure, she was annoyed with him for being a needless jerk to her good friend, but at least she understood it.

To Sebastian, she gave a slight nod and said, "You'll understand if I don't bother to shake your hand."

With that, she boarded the dinghy and departed, leaving both men in the doghouse until further notice.

Topher decided he needed to get back to the focused Topher—the one finishing up his degree and working on the reef sustainability project—and to stop worrying about women and to definitely not partake of any more herbal substances with his friend. He was going to have his escapism in the undersea world that felt like home to him, where no one gave him grief, nothing caused any problems, and he could be happy and carefree.

Pippa, meanwhile, woke up in the worst of moods. Aside from the monster headache throbbing at the base of her skull, she was so damned mad at herself for ever having let herself have feelings for Topher.

"God, what was I even thinking, leaving your brother's wedding with him that night?" she said to Zander as she dug into her French toast piled high with strawberries, blueberries, and heated maple syrup. "Honestly, nothing like overeating to satiate a hangover. Feed a hangover, starve a fever, isn't that what they say?"

Zander looked at her, deadpan. "Pretty sure it's a cold you feed."

"But seriously, why would I have sex with my best friend's brother? I mean is that not a recipe for disaster?"

Zander shrugged. "Maybe because the mood struck you?"

"Yeah, but I'm more disciplined than that," she said. "You know that guy I started to talk about last night. What's-his-name. I mean how long did he try to get into my pants? But I refused to let him. I thought I was simply being selective. But maybe I'm just a cold-hearted woman, unable to bond with men."

"Yep," he said. "I have long said that about you. Pippa, the one who would come running if someone skinned their knee. Pippa, the one who sat with Isabella all night when she broke up with her first love. Pippa who

Love Is in the Heir

didn't even want to own up to what she saw when she walked in on Topher that time because she didn't want to hurt his feelings. *That*, folks, is cold-hearted Pippa at her finest."

"Fine, so sometimes I can be nice," she said. "But then why doesn't Topher like me?"

"You do know you sound like a whiny schoolgirl complaining because the boy she's got a crush on didn't pass a note to her during class."

"And nobody ever passed me notes during class," Pippa said as she started to cry for the umpteenth time in the past twenty-four hours. "I'm unlovable."

By the time the private jet touched down in Monaforte, Zander was exhausted from being the dutiful bestie to Pippa. He'd arranged to hand her off to Clem at the airport.

"Tag, you're it," he said to Clementine practically the minute his feet hit the tarmac. "You've created this monster. Now you have to figure out how to care for her."

I didn't create anything," she said. "I only encouraged what seemed natural."

"Yeah, well, snakebites are natural too, but it doesn't mean you want to lie down in a pit full of them."

"Keep working on your metaphors," she said.

Pippa was a minute behind Zander getting off the plane, lingering longer than she maybe should have.

"Pips, come on," he said. "Clem's going to take you home now."

"I'm kind of savoring my last moments on the jet," she

said. "Not likely I'll be on it again, since things didn't work out with me and Topher."

Zander rolled his eyes. "You're still my friend. You're still a close family friend. You're not being barred from future flights. Hell, you've been on about a thousand vacations with us over the years. I'm pretty sure you'll be on one again sometime in your lifetime."

Pippa started to cry. Again. Thinking about a lifetime without anyone to love her.

Clem took one look at her friend's swollen face and grabbed her hand.

"There, there, sweetie," she said. "Everything's going to be fine. I've stocked your fridge, there's ice cream and chicken soup and wine. Lots and lots of wine. Everything you'll need to get over a dumb boy."

"Is there a puppy?"

Clementine knit her brow. "A puppy?"

Pippa nodded. "I think a puppy would help me get over a boy."

Clem shrugged. "Very well. If you think a puppy's gonna cure what ails you, then by all means, let's do it."

Clementine turned toward Zander. "You owe me one for this, you know."

"Count on it," he said. "Next time you want a flight to the BVI, consider it done," he said, laughing, then gave Pippa a big hug right before he got into his car and waved good-bye.

Chapter Twenty-Three

TOPHER had been floating all day. His version of a spa treatment. If anything would clear his mind, it was the freedom of being suspended in warm, tropical waters. He'd been swimming and snorkeling in and around the Indian islands, an archipelago of islets, really only rock outcroppings, practically within shouting distance of Tortola. The reefs at the Indians were teaming with fish, and his efforts had paid off. Nestled amidst the sea fans and other coral, he saw puffer fish, barracuda, two Anegada lobsters, schools of striped jacks, black-banded porkfish, and the distinctly striped sergeant majors galore. An eagle ray glided past, and he marveled at the grace and beauty of the creature. He kicked his flippers a little quicker to get away from a nearby moray eel; he knew a bite from that would be extremely painful and likely to fester, so he steered clear. Topher was wise to the relatively few dangers that existed in this tropical paradise.

A cheerful-looking green turtle meandered by, which made Topher smile. It was nice to smile after the week he'd had, mostly spent ruminating on what had happened between him and Pippa.

And something just kept nagging at him. Why did he feel the need to run? He knew he'd reacted as if he'd touched an electric fence, pulling back so immediately. He couldn't quite justify it, either. After all, Pippa was pretty much perfect for him: she was gorgeous and smart and funny and no-nonsense. He loved a woman who brooked no bullshit from people. Plus his family had long loved her. Pippa was practically one of them.

And why too would he reject her so abruptly, knowing as he did that she'd felt that tang of rejection from her own parents while growing up? How mean was it of him to shun her right as she opened herself up to him?

No two ways about it, he was unable to justify it. It was what it was. Which was why he was gladly escaping his angst in the deep blue sea. Maybe here he'd find the answers he couldn't quite come up with yet.

A school of cobalt-colored blueheads swam by, just as a trumpet fish swam perpendicular to the sea floor, seemingly suspended in midfloat. Some lone angelfish appeared here and there, flitting about between sea fans and colorful coral formations. He always thought they should be called Swedish fish, with their bright blue-and-yellow coloring like the Swedish flag.

He looked down to see a spotted eagle ray, its beautiful coloring a stark contrast to the sea floor. He soon saw a school of prehistoric-looking silvery bonefish, looking like they'd only recently emerged from the primordial ooze. And right when he was admiring a brilliant school of blue tang, he saw fish scatter in all directions and the place seemed suddenly deserted.

He looked out of the corner of his mask to see why: a juvenile lemon shark, zigging and zagging ominously through the reef. It got his heart racing having a shark nearby even though he knew lemon sharks were relatively harmless and thus he wasn't on that fish's menu. He felt pretty safe in these Caribbean waters. It felt to him like he was born there. He knew nothing in these waters would hurt him.

Love Is in the Heir

Pippa and Clementine were curled up on the sofa in her living room. The cold October chill outside seemed merely a harbinger of the cold, dark winter that was fast approaching, so Pippa gladly took advantage of the nip in the air to build a fire in the large fireplace. Since she'd returned from her trip, she was seeking out anything that would make her feel more at home and cozy. Which meant it was a perfect time to whip up a batch of rich, thick, European-style hot chocolate. They drank it while deep in conversation.

"Hate to even bring up the dreaded subject, but... any word from Toph?" Clementine said.

Pippa shook her head. "Nope. But then again, I hadn't expected to hear from him. He made it abundantly clear I was off the list."

Clementine half laughed. "Yeah, I guess that handshake sort of spoke volumes."

"Handshake," Pippa said with a huff. "I mean, seriously. Was that the weirdest thing or what? Who does that?"

They both got a laugh out of that, because, yeah, it was about the strangest way to blow off a woman, especially one you'd been intimate with only half a day earlier.

"But I'm doing okay with it," Pippa said. "The more I've mulled this over, the more I realize it was just a stupid fling and could never be more than that. I mean what are the chances that the two of us hooking up would ever be anything more than a casual thing, right? Which would have only made it ultimately more awkward to be around Zander and the family. And really, they're like a second family to me, so why would I jeopardize that for a go-nowhere relationship that would only eventually make me angry? And of course we'd then break up, and then how would I be part of the family events at the palace I've always joined them for?"

Clementine nodded. "You could always hang with my family, you know?"

"Of course I do, Clem," she said. "And I really appreciate it a lot. I love you all to bits. And maybe this year I'll celebrate Christmas with you, assuming Topher's back by then. Who knows? He's been absent for a lot of things over the past few years, so it's possible he won't be back. Plus things might be a little, well, tender for me, emotionally, to be there this year. So keep a seat warm for me on Christmas Eve, just in case, 'kay?"

"You got it. Though as much as I'd love for you to be there, it might be smarter for you to get back in the saddle. You know what I mean? The longer you wait, the harder it might be to reintegrate yourself there."

"That's true," Pippa said. "But the other thing is everyone is pairing up in Zander's family now. First Adrian and now Z and Andi. At some point, I'm going to start feeling like a fifth wheel anyhow."

"So when that happens, how about you and I use that as a chance to take an exotic vacation together? Maybe we do a safari or something."

Pippa smiled. "Sorry, Clem, but I've already done the safari thing. I'm in Africa so much for work that it's my favorite diversion when there. Maybe we can do something like the Fiji Islands."

"Or Australia," Clem said. "I've never been. I hear it's gorgeous."

Love Is in the Heir

"Throw in a kangaroo or a koala bear, and I'm all over that," she said. "Plus it would be their summer so we could be warm and get suntanned. Or maybe we can go to China and see the panda bears. I've always wanted to hold a baby panda."

Clem put her hand on her friend's knee. "I can't tell you how glad I am to see that you're moving on and not dwelling on this."

She reached around to set her mug down, and her elbow accidentally hit Pippa in the boob.

"Ow," Pippa said. "That hurt!"

Clementine shrugged. "Sorry! Didn't mean to do that."

"Don't worry about it. Normally that wouldn't have bothered me at all, but for some reason my boobs have been killing me lately."

"Huh. Weird."

"Yeah, it's probably because I've been super careful about taking my birth control every morning now, so the hormones are messing with me more."

Clementine glanced at her out of the side of her eyes. "Huh. Yeah."

"So I decided to get a puppy after all," Pippa said. "Zander had a good point. It will be a good distraction for me. And I love puppies. And they love you unconditionally, which is a great change from certain humans. You wanna come with me to pick her up?"

"As long as you promise to let me babysit her when you have to leave town for work!"

"You're tops on my babysitting list, always."

Which Pippa was starting to fear would only ever be for the four-legged variety, what with her history of failed relationships.

Chapter Twenty-Four

TOPHER hung up the phone, still reeling from his fantastic news. He was so excited he even woke Sebastian, who was not exactly a morning person.

"Dude, get up," Topher said. "We're headed to Oz."

"Huh? What?" Sebastian said, rubbing his eyes. "Stop. The. Light," he said, pointing at the door, letting in too much bright daylight.

"I got it," Topher said. "The research project near the Great Barrier Reef. They agreed to let me sign on to work, and I can use it for my final three independent study credits," he said. "Then I'm done with school."

Sebastian blinked his eyes repeatedly, squinting against the brightness.

"Way to go, my man," he said. "You need someone to sail with you who knows the area?"

"Well, no kidding," Topher said. "I wouldn't go without you. I kind of feel like we've become a team."

"Let's do it," he said, rolling out of bed and rubbing his stomach before stretching his arms and yawning. "I can have a sailboat tricked out for us and lined up by the end of the day if you take care of booking our flights."

"I'm on it," Topher said. "And, uh, take care of that thing, would you?" he said, pointing at his friend's morning wood.

"Wouldn't have been a problem if you hadn't stopped me from going back to that girl's boat last night."

"Yeah, and leaving me stranded at Foxy's? Thanks, but

Love Is in the Heir

no thanks," he said. "Now go. We've got a lot to do to get out of here."

Weeks later, Topher was anchored near shore half a world away, drinking a Foster's and staring at the most amazing sunset he'd likely ever seen when his phone rang.

"Christ, you're hard to get hold of," Zander said. "Where the hell are you?"

Topher took a swig of his beer. "Paradise, brother. Paradise."

"You already were in paradise," he said. "How could it get any better?"

"Seriously," he said. "This is kind of the British Virgin Islands on steroids when it comes to an incredible underwater world."

"Do you ever plan to get home? Or are you just a wandering spirit now?"

"I might be able to get back there by Christmas, if you're lucky."

"Don't do us any favors."

"Trust me, I won't. If it works out, I'll be back, but if something better comes along..."

"And I thought I had commitment problems. But you take the cake."

"I haven't got commitment issues."

"Uh, one word: Pippa," Zander said.

"Ouch," Topher said. "That was below the belt."

"Only calling it as I see it," he said. "And by the way, thanks a lot for leaving me to be the hazmat cleanup crew on that one."

Jenny Gardiner

Topher frowned. "Was it bad?"

"Was it bad? Is the sky blue?"

"Sometimes."

"Seriously, Toph. You have to admit you were a bit of a dick with her."

He nodded his head, taking another swig of beer. "Yeah, yeah, I know. And I'm sorry about that. I froze. I didn't know what to do. We were all stuck on that tiny boat, and I couldn't do it."

"Even though it was your own doing."

"I know. I was a complete asshole and I deserve your wrath. I deserve *her* wrath. And I feel awful about it. But it's probably better. You know me, I'm not one to stick around."

"Yeah, well, maybe you should work on that. It's fine to wander, but at some point you have to figure out what makes you keep running."

Topher squinted his eyes. "I'm not running away from anything. I'm totally running toward things. It's a big world out here. I'm just eating it up."

"Yeah, well, in your haste to run toward something, maybe you can think about who you're hurting and leaving behind. I know one woman who suffered for it."

"Damn, Zander. I already felt bad enough about it. You're not helping matters."

"Dude. I'm calling it like I see it," he said. "Pippa has been my closest friend since forever, and I hate to see her hurting."

"She's still upset about things? It's been like six weeks. I figured she'd be well and truly over me by now."

"Don't flatter yourself that she's sitting home pining for you," his brother said. "She's been traveling for the foundation. So she's been busy. But I know you probably set her back relationshipwise for a long time. It's a good thing she got a puppy, because I can't see her bonding over much else for a good while."

For some reason that made Topher feel slightly happy to know Pippa wasn't with another guy. Which was entirely selfish of him. But the idea of her with someone else roiled his stomach. For whatever reason, he wasn't prepared to keep her in his life, but he also wasn't ready to watch her start anew with someone else. And yeah, he knew that he was a total dick for wanting to have it both ways.

"So, yeah, I'll stay in touch and let you know if I can make it back for Christmas," Topher said, feeling the need to get off the call. "Give Mum my love, and give Bella a squeeze."

It was definitely easier for Topher to shut out his other life than to figure out what he was actually afraid of. And he knew he'd need to figure that one out. Someday.

Chapter Twenty-Five

"I need you to get over here like, yesterday," Pippa texted to Clementine. "I'm talking faster than the speed of light. Hurry!"

Clementine tried to call as soon as she got the message, but the calls went straight to voice mail.

She pulled up to Pippa's house and raced inside, but Pippa was nowhere to be found.

"Pips!" she called as she wandered from room to room. She even checked the home theater, but it was empty.

Finally she found Pippa, curled up in a ball in her huge walk-in closet, her black Labrador puppy, Muffin, clutched in her arms, tears pouring down, and a plastic stick in her hand.

"Honey," Clem said, racing over to give her a hug. "What can be this wrong?"

"Pink." Pippa said through loud wails.

"What?"

"It's pink," she bawled.

"What's pink?"

"The stick," Pippa said, gasping for air between her incessant crying jags. "It's pink."

Clementine stared at the stick, and it started to sink in. "Oh crap and a half. Topher."

Pippa nodded hard.

"Baby."

Pippa nodded.

Love Is in the Heir

"Fuck."

Pippa nodded especially hard.

"But I thought everything was fine," Clem said. "You didn't tell me you were having any problems. Wouldn't you have been getting sick or something?"

Pippa frowned.

"You were getting sick?"

She nodded.

"And you didn't tell me?"

"It's called deep denial," Pippa said, her sobs subsiding momentarily. "I think I thought if I ignored it, it wouldn't be true. I mean what are the chances?"

Clementine pursed her lips. "I'd say pretty good, judging by that stupid pink stick."

Pippa started to cry again.

"I can't be pregnant," she said. "I can barely take care of a puppy who wakes me up every night. What would I do with a baby?"

"At least a baby won't have sharp puppy teeth."

"If you're trying to make me laugh, it's not working," Pippa said. "Plus at least a puppy turns into a self-sufficient dog in a short period of time. A baby is like, forever. I'll have this thing needing me till I'm ninety!"

Clementine laughed lightly. "Maybe not that long, sweetie," she said. "But yeah, a baby is needy. No question about that."

"What the hell am I going to do?"

"For starters, have you told Topher?"

Pippa shook her head. "God, no. Are you kidding me? He shook my damned hand. I'd say he pretty much has no interest in being anything in my life."

"Yeah, but a baby is a game changer," she said.

"I'm not having any part in forcing myself on the man simply because one stupid damned sperm of his got drunk over cocktails with an overzealous egg of mine and they took it too far. That, my friend, is no reason to force a man who made it abundantly clear he wasn't interested in a relationship into a relationship. For bleeding ever."

She started to cry again.

"Gosh, Pips, how long have you known something was wrong?"

She shook her head. "I don't know. I think I must've known for a few weeks things weren't right. Remember I said my boobs were killing me? And then I got so damned tired. And then wine—wine!—started to taste horrible. I mean I can't imagine a scenario for me that wine would taste horrible. And then I started throwing up."

"Oh, Pippa," Clementine said, giving her a hug. "What can I do to help out?"

She shrugged. "Hell if I know," she said. "I don't know the first thing about pregnancy, let alone a baby."

"Have you told anyone?"

"Not a soul. Nor will I. Until I have no choice in the matter."

"At some point you owe it to Topher to let him know."

She shook her head. "Honestly, it will only make it harder for me to get re-rejected by the guy. I mean the great news is I can afford to do this on my own, you know? Think about how many women don't have that luxury."

Clementine nodded.

"And I've got plenty of room around here," she said, spreading her arms out. "I mean not like my folks are ever here. For that matter, I could probably raise a child and

Love Is in the Heir

never even see the thing in this place."

"I like your attitude with this, Pips. So let's start looking at some more pros, here," Clementine said, enumerating with her fingers. "First, it's not like you're a teenager. You're plenty old enough to be a responsible mum."

"I was fast approaching being too old, for that matter."

"Oh, stop," she said. "And you have so much love in you. Look how much you adore this puppy."

"Yeah, but the puppy has soft fur. I love soft fur."

"I'm sure your baby will have some attribute that will attract you to it with equal fervor."

Pippa shrugged. "Hard to imagine. I'm a big fan of baby animals, but baby people? I don't have the slightest idea what you do with them."

"Well, neither do I. But we can figure that out. I'm sure there must be books."

"I'm too tired to read."

"Okay. Well, we'll deal with that later. So how about this is a chance for you to reinvent yourself from a family perspective. Make up for where your parents went wrong. You can be the mother you never had."

"*And* the father," Pippa said, tears welling up in her eyes as she stroked her puppy.

"You'll be the best father with a vagina that there's ever been," Clementine said, which at least elicited a laugh from her friend. "And you'll finally be rooted to a family, your very own family, once this baby comes, so even if you have to raise it on your own, it's okay. After all, like you said, you're blessed to have the resources to do that. You might not have had a lot of overt love in your family growing up, but at least now you have family money to help when you're gonna need it most."

Pippa gave her a hug. "If you came here to cheer me up, you're doing a pretty damned good job of it. Curse you."

"It's what you pay me the big bucks for," she said. "Now, let's start practicing to be a good mum by feeding this puppy some dinner. She's gnawing on my fingers, so she must be starving."

"Fine," Pippa said. "But if I need a substitute husband to help out, can I count on you?"

Clem smiled. "I already promised you I'd be your forever babysitter, didn't I?" she said. "I didn't realize I was going to have to watch an actual baby so soon, but that's okay!"

"I can live without a man, but I could never live without my best friend," Pippa said, giving her another hug as she picked herself up, dusted herself off, and dropped that cursed pink stick in the wastebasket.

Chapter Twenty-Six

TOPHER and Sebastian were hours from their home base in Airlie Beach, navigating around shallow reefs in the Whitsunday Islands where Topher had been tasked with checking on tagged tortoises, which was a bit like searching for a needle in a haystack.

"What say we take the rest of the day off and head over to Whitehaven Beach," Sebastian said. The beach was famous for its gleaming white sand that combined with a multitude of shades of aqua water to create an almost portrait-like swirl of unsurpassed natural beauty. Hundreds of thousands of tourists each year sought out the breathtaking pristine scenery of the protected Whitehaven Beach.

They anchored a few hundred yards out and motored onto the beach on the dinghy. The sand was so white it was nearly blinding in the brilliant midday sun. As they wandered onto the shore, Topher couldn't believe how soft the nearly pure silica sand was. The place was teeming with birds and butterflies and crabs skittering about. The wildlife combined with the white, white sand set against a brilliant blue sky and crystal clear waters in every shade of azure and turquoise imaginable created an environment that was simply magical.

After a while, they decided to walk into the bush on the island, where they were treated to spying on gargantuan monitor lizards and even a few wallabies. Eventually, they trekked to the Tongue Bay lookout, where they could best view the dramatic ripple effect caused by the shifting sands and tides. The view was impossibly spectacular—truly a natural wonder of the world.

They spent an hour or so hanging out in the shallow waters, relaxing under the warmth of the sun. The water was so clear that from their vantage point they were able to spot green turtles, a lemon shark, and even a graceful ray gliding nearby.

"This sure beats a day job," Sebastian said with a broad grin.

"You're not kidding," Topher said, even though a day job wasn't something he'd have to give very serious consideration to. At some point, royal duties, even for a prince who would likely never be king, would become the expectation for him. But until that time, he was happy to check out of the everyday world in favor of this fantasyland. He would be mercifully spared the duties of a desk job.

As the sun began to get low in the sky, the two men decided to head back to the catamaran for the night, hoping to enjoy sunset from the comfort of the cat's trampoline, cocktails in hand.

Sebastian had boarded the dinghy, and Topher was just about to jump in when he felt something sharp pierce his foot.

"Crap, that hurt," he said to Sebastian, assuming he'd stepped on a broken shell, or maybe a crab had pinched him. But within seconds a debilitating pain inched its way from his foot, through his calf, past his thigh, and within minutes was coursing its way through his entire body. He had no idea what had happened, but never could he imagine pain like this, and he knew he'd stepped on

Love Is in the Heir

something deadly.

"Get help fast!" he screamed to Sebastian, who pulled him the rest of the way into the dinghy and sped out to the boat. Once there, he contacted emergency services on the satellite phone.

Meanwhile, Topher was writhing in complete agony, screaming as if someone was gutting him from the inside out.

"Toph, man, hang tight," Sebastian said, wringing his hands. "They'll get here as soon as they can."

Topher's body became rigid, his eyes wide with terror. His screams pierced the silence that had till then only been broken by seabirds and water lapping at the boat. He lapsed in and out of consciousness.

"Sebastian," he choked out. "Do something. Knock me out so I can't feel this pain anymore. I can't take any more of it. I'd sooner die than have to experience one more second."

Sebastian grabbed his hand and held tight. "Toph, I don't know what I can do, but I have to try to keep you awake. The emergency medical folks said it was crucial I not let you pass out."

"I'm fucking dying. And I'm not exaggerating. Please, I'm begging you. Just kill me and get it over with." Topher's cries could likely be heard for miles, carried over the open water above the sound of waves or motors or squalling gulls.

It took what seemed a lifetime for the helicopter to arrive and get out to the boat. Immediately, they administered a shot of morphine to stop the pain and three shots of pain medicine in his foot to lessen the torturous pain at the site of whatever this sting was. His foot had swollen three times its size and looked like it belonged to a cartoon character.

Soon Topher was deeply sedated and stabilized enough to be evacuated to a hospital. Sebastian had to stay behind to deal with the sailboat and take care of reaching out to Topher's family.

He wasn't looking forward to that call, and it would be hours till he could join Topher at the hospital, the whole time not knowing if he'd be alive by the time he got there.

He wasn't even sure whom to contact but decided Zander would be his go-to man, so he called him first.

"Z, it's Sebastian," he said, his voice shaking with nerves.

"Sebastian! What is up?"

"I'm really sorry to call you," he said. "I don't even know if I'm waking you up. But I wanted to be sure you knew so you and your family could get here immediately."

"You all right?"

"It's Topher."

"What happened?"

"We were having a perfect day in the most perfect place on the planet," he said. "He was pushing the dinghy into deeper water and was about to jump on board when he stepped on something. Something venomous. The emergency medical team is pretty sure it's called a cone snail. It's a type of snail that launches a deadly poison-filled spear at its prey. And unfortunately, it thought your brother's foot was dinner."

"Is he there with you?"

"He just got medevaced out to hospital," Sebastian said. "I couldn't go with him; no room on the helicopter, plus I have to deal with this sailboat. But he's not doing

Love Is in the Heir

well, Zander. I don't know if he's going to live through the night."

"Fuck," Zander said. "Listen, text me everything I need to know. I've got to get hold of my family and notify them all so we can leave immediately."

"Hurry, Zander. I don't know if he can last."

Zander wasted no time tracking down his entire family, and they were headed to the airport in record time. But right before he left the palace, he knew he had one more call to make.

"Pips," he said when she picked up the phone. "Come quick. There's been a bad accident. I'm not sure if Topher will live through the night. We're flying out within the hour. Meet us at the airport."

One last thing Zander took care of en route to the airport: he had to get his mother and father up to speed on the Topher-Pippa romance, so that no one questioned the need for her to be there for this dire emergency. His brother was going to need all the support they could muster.

Chapter Twenty-Seven

PIPPA couldn't focus. Everything was swirling in her mind: Topher. Accident. Near death. What the hell? This was completely impossible. And where was he even? And who was *we*? Was the entire family going to be there? If so, why would they want Pippa? The last thing Topher needed was her coming along for the ride.

But Zander was certain when he said it, no doubt about it.

She threw a few things in a bag, called Clem to come get the puppy, grabbed her car keys, and left. She took the cliffside curves from her home toward the airport ridiculously fast, but no way was she going to miss this flight.

At the airport, she was diverted to the tarmac where the largest of the royal jets stood waiting, and a flight attendant immediately ushered her on board.

She raced up the steps, out of breath, and arrived to see the entire family there: Queen Ariana, her eyes swollen from crying; her husband, Prince Enrico, who held her in his arms; Adrian and his new wife, Emma; Zander and his serious girlfriend, Andi; Isabella and Luca. Everyone but Topher, who was lying somewhere—she didn't even know where—in a hospital bed, fighting for his life.

Ariana rushed to Pippa and wrapped her in her arms. "Pippa, dear, we're so glad you could make it," she said, dabbing at her damp eyes with a tissue. "I know Christopher will be so happy to see you."

Love Is in the Heir

Christopher would be thrilled to see her? And how did the queen know that? Was there a lot of information shared that she wasn't aware of?

She looked over at Zander, her brows furrowed.

"Sorry, Pips," he said. "I had to spill all. Toph needs all the support he can get right now."

Pippa gulped. Good thing Zander didn't know "all." Clearly this was not the time to share that surprising news with them.

"Can someone fill me in on what happened?" she said. "I don't even know where Toph is, let alone what happened to him."

Ariana motioned for everyone to sit down, and the group settled into the plush leather furniture in the living room area of the jet as the captain announced the plane was ready for departure.

"I got a call from Sebastian about ninety minutes ago," Zander said. "I knew they'd flown off to Australia a few weeks ago for some project Toph got invited to participate in. He said he'd only do it if Sebastian would come along and skipper the boat for him."

"Thank God he was with him," Ariana said.

"Indeed. There are a lot of things we can thank our lucky stars for," Enrico said, rubbing his wife's shoulders to comfort her. She pressed her hand to his in gratitude. The two of them were so sweet together even after all these years, Pippa thought. She envied the closeness of this family. Sure they were the Firm, which from the outside could almost come across as a corporate entity, but more important than that, they were family. She could feel tears welling in her eyes, which she quickly wiped away with her hand. She chalked up her weepiness to those rushing hormones that had invaded her body in spades of late.

"Sebastian said Toph had been in calf-deep water near the shore when he felt something supersharp pierce his foot," Zander said. "He thought maybe he'd stepped on a shell, but instantly the pain started to resonate throughout his body."

"Poor Topher," Pippa said. "What was it?"

"It's called a cone snail—"

"Wait, a *snail*? He's lying in a hospital bed near death due to a scrawny little mollusk?"

"This is no regular snail," Adrian said. "Google it. One type of cone snail is jokingly called the 'cigarette snail' because you have only enough time to smoke one before you die from the venom."

Pippa's eyes got as large as saucers. "You mean he could've been dead before they even got him to a hospital?"

Ariana nodded her head and started to cry out loud. Enrico pulled her into his arms, stroking her hair to soothe her. Pippa wished she had Topher here to stroke her hair right about now.

"How could this thing be so deadly?" she said.

Zander shrugged. "The bastard's weaponized, from what I've read. It launches a venom-laden, harpoon-like missile at its victims, who never even have a chance since the snail detects motion and indiscriminately fires the thing."

"Worse still, it can deliver a mix of a hundred different neurotoxins so complex there is no antivenom. It can cause paralysis, or it can make your heart stop pumping and your lungs stop breathing," Luca said. "Or it can make all your muscles contract once. Said to be indescribably painful."

Love Is in the Heir

"It's like that horrible Cruciatus Curse in *Harry Potter*. Only courtesy of Mother Nature instead of Voldemort," Isabella said, and Luca threw her a WTF look.

"What can I say?" Isabella said. "I love those books!"

"Here," Zander said, tossing his phone to Pippa. "Look at this video we found online."

Pippa pressed play and watched as this harmless-looking sea snail launched its venom-filled harpoon, killing its prey in a split second. It made her stomach churn to watch. So much so that she quickly covered her mouth. Only that wasn't going to do the trick, so she suddenly got up and raced to the bar sink nearby, just in time to throw up in it.

Ariana was quick to rush to her aid. "Are you all right, sweetheart?" she said, reaching for a dishtowel to moisten under the water. She placed it over Pippa's forehead, then walked her back to her seat.

"Jeez, Pips, weak stomach much?" Zander said. "Next I can show you some shark-attack footage with blood-filled waters just to see how you react if you'd like."

"Zander," his mother said.

"Merely trying to cut the tension in the plane, Mum," he said. "We're all on edge and worried about Toph. Figured I'd take the piss for us all."

"I'm so sorry for that," Pippa said, wiping her brow. "I don't know what came over me. But watching that creature in action... My God, it seems like quite the overkill for a stupid little snail, doesn't it? If he wants to kill a bloody fish, why on earth does he have to use a nuclear bomb on the thing? Can't he have a little net pop out or something? Poor Toph couldn't even get injured by something more grandiose, like a great white shark. Had to be a damned snail."

They all laughed, which was a good thing to break up some of the tension.

"So where is Topher now, and how's he doing?" she asked.

"He's in hospital in Queensland," Isabella said. "He was rushed there by helicopter."

"They've got him on heavy doses of morphine," Enrico added. "All they can do is try to diminish the pain and hope for the best."

Until that moment, the magnitude of what happened hadn't quite hit Pippa. But when it did, it came in a rush, and she began to bawl.

"You mean I could lose Topher and I didn't even fight for him?" she said through choking tears. Zander pulled her into his arms and held her and let her cry. "I'm such an idiot. I knew I could have pushed it with him, but I wanted to be just as stubborn as he was being. I knew he didn't want to send me away, but his stupid pride took the day. I could have fought for him, but no, I wasn't going to be *that* girl. I had too much self-respect to grovel before him."

"It's all right, Phillipa," Ariana said, handing her more tissues. Pips hated that name, but it almost came out as a term of endearment when spoken so kindly by the queen.

"But you don't understand," Pippa sobbed. "It's not all right. I never even told Topher."

"Never told Topher what, darling?" she said.

Pippa looked down at her stomach. "About the baby," she blurted out on the tsunami crest of a loud wail.

Oh lord, Pippa, that wasn't on the agenda, she thought the minute she blurted it out. That took you just about the time it would take a cone snail to shoot its harpoon to

Love Is in the Heir

totally blow your secret, you idiot.

The airplane cabin became suddenly quiet. Even Pippa stopped sobbing in her stupor over her unintended Big Reveal. Hell, she hadn't known if she'd *ever* admit who the father of this baby was, and she sure as hell hadn't planned to announce it to the Queen of Monaforte and her entire bloody family.

Emma stared, bug-eyed, at Adrian, and Andi did the same with Zander. The rest of the family cast glances at one another, stunned into silence. Finally Ariana spoke.

"You're pregnant with Christopher's baby?"

There were all sorts of things that were triggering Pippa's unsettled stomach these days, and nerves certainly were a factor. Which is why she once more raced to the sink to throw up.

"I'm so very sorry," she said. "I don't want to make the sink disgusting. Really, I don't."

Ariana was back at her side in a flash. "Honey, you're pregnant with our grandchild?"

Pippa's lip jutted out in a pout. "Yes," she said as she started to cry all over again.

The entire family sat looking at one another, not knowing quite what to do or say.

It was going to be a long flight.

Chapter Twenty-Eight

POOR Pippa was exhausted. But the family had questions, and they deserved answers. Especially considering their son and brother could well be dead by the time they arrived there. As much as she was yearning to simply pass out on the comfy leather sofa, maybe even with her head in her bestie Zander's lap, Andi permitting, she knew she had to start from the beginning and explain everything. Some of which at least Ariana must have known. And of course Luca, being that he saw her sneaking out of the palace that morning following Adrian's wedding.

"Can I gloss over the details, maybe?" she asked, her face turning red from embarrassment.

They all nodded, though Luca had to put in his two cents' worth.

"Hell no," he said. "The details are the most compelling part, usually."

Pippa smirked at him and continued.

"Very well, then. So Topher and I have known each other for a long time," she started.

"Cut to the chase, Pips," Zander said. "No need in stating the obvious. After all, we don't have all night."

"Well, actually, we do," Adrian said, looking at his watch. "This is going to be a long damned flight."

"This is like settling in to watch a good movie," Isabella said, curling her legs up under her. "I wish I had some popcorn."

"Did someone say they'd like popcorn?" the flight

attendant asked, then mouthed 'sorry' in case she was being disruptive. Or nosy by listening in. She went to heat up popcorn in the microwave oven in the galley.

"Oh, good lord, welcome to my sideshow," Pippa muttered. "So Topher and I got a little carried away at Adrian's wedding," she said. "Let's leave it at that."

Luca nodded, attesting to having witnessed the aftermath.

"And then I realized it was a mistake, so let's just say I wasn't reciprocating any attempts at repeating events of that night. It didn't help matters that Zander was giving poor Toph a heap of crap for everything."

His mother threw him a stern look. "Didn't we talk about your leaving Topher alone?" she said to him.

"Yes, Mum," Zander said, hanging his head in faux shame.

"I mean it. I want you to stop with the teasing. You know Christopher has always been sensitive to that sort of thing. It's time to leave him well enough alone!"

"Listen to your mother," Pippa said to Zander, wrinkling her brow. "Okay, so then Clementine, Darcy's sister, tricked me into going to the British Virgin Islands, delivering me right to Topher's damned boat before I even knew where I was going."

Isabella raised her hand. "Uh, how could you not know where you were going? Did you not notice the islands below from the airplane? What about the signs at the airport?"

"She blindfolded me. I swear it. I hadn't a clue."

"What a lovely gesture," Ariana said. "Helping her friend out like that."

"Yeah, well, I don't know about that," Pippa said. "I'd

say more like annoying."

"So then what?" Emma said. "This story sounds so romantic. Unrequited love, missed cues. I can't wait to hear how it ends."

Which might not have been the best comment to make, considering that the hero of the story was under heavy sedation in a hospital bed at the moment. She covered her mouth and whispered *sorry* to everyone. Ariana patted her on the knee to let her know it was fine.

"So I tried—really I tried, hard—to resist Topher," she said. "But at some point the man really is irresistible." She smiled, remembering how very irresistible he was.

"But then Zander showed up. It was all innocently enough, believe it or not," she said. "But the timing couldn't have been worse, and all sorts of problems ensued, and the whole thing spooked Topher out quite a bit. Enough so that the next day he shook my hand and said good-bye. Mentioned something about being like a turtle that travels far from his family, not meant to be near them or some such nonsense."

"Wait a minute," Luca said. "You spent the night with him at the palace. You clearly spent the night with him on the boat. And the next day he kicks you to the curb with nothing but a handshake? What is wrong with him?"

"Seriously," Pippa said, rolling her eyes. "I was so mad, I figured to hell with him. If he wanted to behave like a stupid child, then so be it."

"And you haven't seen him since then?" Ariana said.

Pippa shrugged and shook her head, pursing her lips. "Nope," she said. "And then, well, I got sort of busy. What with throwing up ten times a day. Not to mention freaking out because a baby wasn't exactly on my to-do list for

Love Is in the Heir

forever. I mean what do I know about being a mother? My own parents were best at *not* being parents. And they were my role models. This poor child is doomed."

Ariana took Pippa's hand in hers. "Silly girl," she said. "You'll be a divine mother. Do you know how much you mothered all my children when you were all little?"

Pippa shook her head.

"You made sure everyone picked up their toys when you were done playing," Ariana continued. "You made them clear their dishes after meals. You reminded them of my birthday each year. You told them to mind their manners when they burped at the dinner table. And do you remember when Nero, our black cocker spaniel, died? You comforted my children as much if not more than I did. Pippa Grimaldi, your baby will be lucky to call you Mum."

Which launched Pippa into a downright squall of tears, all happy, except for the black cloud of unknown about Topher hovering overhead.

"So you're not mad at me?" Pippa said.

"Oh, heavens no, dear girl," Ariana said, smiling at Enrico, who was nodding his head. "We're quite ecstatic, in fact. We're going to be grandparents! And you, young lady, are carrying our grandbaby, so let's get you off to bed so you can get some rest. It's been a stressful, long day."

Before she knew it, Pippa was being tucked into bed by none other than the Queen of Monaforte, who stroked her forehead and kissed her on the cheek. Like a real mother would do. Not a bad way to end a very bad day.

Chapter Twenty-Nine

THE whole lot of them were run ragged by the time their jet landed at the small airport in Northern Queensland and a limousine rushed them to the nearby hospital.

Ariana rushed to her son's side, nearly knocking down a nurse to get there as quickly as possible. "I'm sorry, love," she said to the woman. "Please forgive my manners. I simply need to see that my boy is all right."

The nurse smiled. "No worries. I completely understand. He took quite a nick, this one did."

"Honestly, I'm going to lock him in his room from here on out so he's safe," Ariana said, reaching for her son's hand, which was taped up with IV needles. "It's your mum, baby," she said. "You're going to be okay."

Topher lay there for what seemed forever, his face contorted from the ongoing pain, despite the heavy doses of pain meds flowing through his body. In the background were sobs from Ariana and Pippa, who tucked herself into the far corner of the room. The rest of the group stood there, staring at the monitors that were recording Topher's vitals, reassuring his family that he was indeed still alive.

Soon Toph began to stir, tossing from side to side, moaning, and eventually his eyes opened ever so gradually.

"Hey, mate," Zander said, leaning over his brother. "Heard you got bit by a butterfly."

Topher's eyes hung heavy, he was so deeply sedated. He tried to talk but nothing came out.

"You gave us all a hell of a scare," Adrian said, holding

Love Is in the Heir

tight to Emma's hand. "You'd better not do something like that ever again or I can assure you Mum will kill you."

"How're you feeling, sweetheart?" his mother asked, her brow creased with worry. "Can I do anything to help you?"

Topher shook his head slightly.

"Meantime we have a little surprise for you," Zander said. "Figured it might cheer you up a bit."

Luca stepped aside as Pippa emerged from the back of the room. She approached the bed feeling awkward and gangly and hating being the center of attention.

Topher's eyes opened wider, and he tried to mouth her name but all he seemed to do was form the letter "P" with his mouth.

She put her finger to his lips to quiet him. "Shhhh," she said. "Don't talk. You have to save your energy to get better."

He moved his hand slowly toward her, and she reached for it, clasping it between both of hers as she pulled it to her, pressing her lips to his fingertips. Her eyes filled with tears.

"Hey," she said quietly.

She looked up, and everyone was staring at them. She moved her head in the direction of the door, hoping they'd all take the hint and give them a few moments of privacy. The family filed out of the room one by one, and Ariana, the last one out, respectfully closed the door behind her.

"Topher, I'm so sorry this happened to you," she said through the tears. "I can't tell you how mad I am at myself for having let you ditch me. That was so not cool of you, by the way. Ever since that day, I've thought about you more times than I care to remember. I don't want to say you were haunting my thoughts, but... Actually, damn you, you'd really have haunted my thoughts if you had died before we had a chance to talk. Toph, look, I know it matters to you, this whole thing about how your brothers give you a hard time. I get that. I know you're sensitive to appearances. I mean, who's not? But maybe you more so than some men. I don't know. But T, we have a lot of fun together. I mean, a lot of fun together. That is, when we decide to not be stupid idiots and avoid each other. And the sex—"

She fanned her face, pretending to be hot and bothered.

"—the sex. I am sure I didn't tell you this, because, well, I didn't want to swell your head or anything, but it was truly the best sex I've ever had. Not that that's saying a whole lot, because it's not as if I've slept with a hundred men, but still. There've been a few. And some, wow, were they not so great. So I do have a good basis of comparison. Like there was this one guy at university—"

Topher tried to clear his throat, and she looked down to see him glaring at her.

She laughed. "Maybe you're starting to improve if that makes you irritated," she said. "Maybe I should start telling you details of every man I've had sex with and see if that will really rev up your engines."

Topher moved his head back and forth slightly.

"I know, I'm not that cruel. After all, the last thing I want to do is upset you. Your family would about kill me. Plus no need in giving you a heart attack. Although I heard this snail thingy's bite is so painful people die from heart attacks. My God, Topher, how the hell did this happen? One drop of venom could kill twenty people! And how did

Love Is in the Heir

you survive it? You poor baby, I'm so sorry."

She leaned down and pressed her lips to his and held them there. She could feel his warm breath against her face, and she felt reassured, as if everything would eventually be fine. Topher was breathing; all was right with the world. Of course, Pippa was a hormonal mess, so this only made the tears come on full force, and as she closed her eyes against them, her tears fell on Topher's face.

She pulled away and wiped at the tears with her thumb right as Topher reached for her hand and pulled it toward him and held tight. With his other hand, he held a thumb up and slowly nodded his head. And only then did Pippa know that things would truly be fine.

Chapter Thirty

TOPHER was released from the hospital by morning, and the entire family plus Sebastian decamped to a luxury resort in the Whitsunday Islands to catch up on sleep and care for their wounded warrior.

Topher wasn't up for much of anything but sleep and watching television. He'd take occasional walks around the pool with Pippa, and they were talking a bit about things, but they weren't getting too intensely into it. He simply didn't have the strength.

She finally persuaded him to sit by the pool with her one afternoon.

"How about slathering on some more sunscreen?" she said, handing him the bottle. We're in the melanoma capital of the world, you know?"

"Seriously?" he asked. "How do you have all these factoids in your head?"

"I just do. Look up there," she said, pointing toward the sky. "There's a huge hole in the ozone layer right up there. The sun is frying the crap out of us as we speak."

Topher grabbed the beer the pool attendant brought to him. "Yeah, well, I think there are more immediate things around here to worry about than that. You stick around this place long enough, I think something's gonna do you in long before the skin cancer does."

Pippa spread her arms out wide, admiring the stunning panorama, with brilliant white sand beaches and water in breathtaking shades of the palest blue green. "How could

Love Is in the Heir

you not fall in love with the beauty of this place?" she said. "I mean look at it."

"Beautiful, sure, but don't move or you're dead," Toph said.

They both laughed, but it was almost too soon for that joke.

"Yeah, maybe Australia is like those brightly colored look-don't-touch tree frogs you see on BBC specials about the rain forest," she said. "The ones that'll kill you within minutes if you come into contact with the venomous secretions on their flesh. Sometimes the prettier the thing is, the more deadly it is. Australia, my friend, is not to be messed with. This place is damned deadly."

Topher leaned over and gave Pippa a soft kiss on the nose.

"I know one very pretty thing that isn't the least bit deadly."

Pippa smiled. "Give me enough time, I could be."

♛

The family had rented out the entire restaurant for their last night at the resort. Ariana wanted to take full advantage of having her entire brood in one place at one time with no outside interruptions.

They sat at a long table set with crystal and china and overflowing flowers, and the late afternoon sun cast a picture-postcard burnished glow on the whole group.

When the waiter finished filling champagne flutes for all, Topher let out a quick whistle and stood up.

"I think an apology is in order," he began.

"For nearly dying on us?" his father said. "All in a

day's work for a parent, son."

"No, for something more than that, Dad," he said. "It took me nearly dying and my family rallying around me for me to realize that at the end of the day, I'm nothing without the big, crazy, sometimes deeply obnoxious, bordering-on-offensive group I'm surrounded with tonight."

They all laughed.

"But seriously," he said. "I think I lost my way a bit back there. I stopped valuing the importance of those I loved." He paused. "Of those I didn't quite realize I loved," he said, nodding toward Pippa. "I guess sometimes it takes something dramatic to snap you out of your lull, and that sure has been the case with me."

"Hear, hear," his mother said, holding up her glass.

"I really want to thank you all for being there for me at a time when I needed it most," he said as he held his glass aloft. "But most importantly, thank you for reminding me about what is most important in life. To love, to life, and to family."

Everyone clapped as they toasted the man they had nearly lost.

Chapter Thirty-One

AFTER dinner, Topher and Pippa strolled hand in hand around the resort. They'd enjoyed yet another spectacular sunset over the water and now watched a full moon rise against an indigo sky.

"I'd say this was a terribly romantic setting but for the fact I'll always associate this place with helping you recover from your near-death experience," she said.

"Does put a slight damper on it, conceptually," he said, giving her nose a little joking pinch.

"Although you do somehow seem to get me to some of the more exquisite settings in the world, one way or another."

"What can I say? If I can't lure you with my charm and good looks, I'll have to take advantage of setting."

"Speaking of setting, so what now for you, Toph? More risking life and limb in pursuit of seagoing creatures?"

He shook his head. "Maybe not with such regularity, at least. I love the ocean, there's no doubt about it, but I'd be lying if I didn't admit that part of the charm for me was getting away from my family and all the duties of being part of this family in particular."

"Those garden parties do get tiring," she said. "But at least you're not going to keel over from them. Unless perhaps a bumblebee stings you and you learn too late you're allergic."

They both laughed.

Jenny Gardiner

"Seriously, though. I finish up in a few weeks, right in time for the holidays."

Pippa didn't want to fish around too much to find out where she stood with Topher's plans, so she remained silent. But hanging over her was the fact that she needed to tell Topher what the rest of his family already knew.

"Penny for your thoughts," he said. "You look like someone just stole your teddy bear."

Pippa dragged her feet as she walked, mimicking how she felt about having this conversation.

"More like I might need a teddy bear," she said, taking a huge breath.

Topher scrunched his brow. "Huh?"

She stopped at a bench along the walkway and sat down, pulling his hand so he followed suit.

"I'm not even sure where to begin, Toph," she said. "But first and foremost, I want you to know that I have no expectations of you. I have enormous feelings for you, but I don't want you to feel like you have to reciprocate them. If you aren't interested in anything long-term with me, that's completely fine. We'll figure it out."

"Figure what out?" Topher said, squinting at her.

Pippa heaved a heavy sigh. "Please, I really don't want you to freak out on me. So promise me you won't."

"I don't even know what I'm not freaking out on, so how could I assure you it's not going to happen?"

"So maybe give me some examples of something that might freak you out."

"You're kidding, right? You want me to start randomly listing things that would upset me a lot?"

"Yeah. Go on. Just for fun."

Topher shook his head. "You're a strange one

Love Is in the Heir

sometimes," he said. "Okay, how about this. If I found out the world was going to end tomorrow. *That* would freak me out."

Pippa nodded. "Fair enough. Go on."

Topher thought for a moment. "Let's see." He held up a finger. "I've got one. If I was swimming with you out there," he pointed to the nearby ocean, "and I saw a big black fin headed toward you. That would *really* freak me out."

"You and me both. Not that the end of the world wouldn't also cause a great deal of panic for me."

"Not to be too morbid, but what would you want to do if you knew today was your last day?" he asked. "Like if the world was going to end tomorrow."

Pippa thought about that, and of course her eyes filled with tears. Because to her that meant that she'd never know the baby she was carrying, and that concept broke her heart. Even more so thinking that Topher would never know about the baby either.

"I think I'd be happy being right here, right now, doing just what we're doing," she said. "How about you?"

"You mean if it was my last day? Well, funny thing, I've had a chance to give that some real thought, what with my nearly having had my last day and not having spent it nearly as wisely as I would have." He turned to face her.

"Well, aside from the deadly sting, it must not have been too bad a day," she said. "I mean, you were here. In paradise. Albeit a deadly paradise, but it beats Siberia."

"It does indeed. Though pretty much everything could probably beat Siberia but for, say, spending time in a prison. But look, Pippa, I'm getting myself all distracted here."

Jenny Gardiner

"I think that's my fault," she said. "I'm failing to disclose something I have to disclose to you."

"Maybe you should come right out and say it."

"You think?"

"I do."

"Okay, but if you freak out, I'm going to run straight to your mum."

Topher laughed. "That sounds like something one of my siblings would have said to me. 'I'm going to go tell Mum!'"

"I adore your mother, Topher," she said. "The thing is, I didn't have a close family. My parents weren't very keen on parenting. They were always gone and leaving me with staff. I mean I didn't even have the luxury of a governess or nanny. Instead it was a succession of maids who took care of our homes and watched me and my brother. And my brother made himself scarce as soon as he was old enough to do so. So I've always loved spending time with your family. Your mother loved on me, and your father gave me fatherly advice, and I got to pretend I was part of that crazy, exhausting group of people who made each other sort of nuts sometimes but ultimately really cared for each other."

"You're right, Pips. They're a great group. I'm so very blessed to have them in my life."

She took a deep breath, placed her hands in his lap, and closed her eyes.

"So I'm going to have a family, Toph. It's not exactly what I'd planned, but I'm excited about it. I'm going to get it right where my parents failed so miserably. And at first it terrified me, but the more I thought about it, the more it thrilled me."

Love Is in the Heir

"Pippa, what are you saying to me?"

"I'm pregnant." She blurted out as she opened her eyes to look at him.

For a minute, the air seemed to leave the room. Insects stopped chirping and the ocean waves grew silent.

Topher's face fell.

"Oh, God, T. I'm so sorry, I knew you'd be so upset about it."

He shook his head. "No, really, Pips, that's great news. Really it is. Congratulations. Who's the lucky man?"

It was Pippa's turn to squint back at Topher. "You're kidding, right?"

"Uh, no. I'm very happy for you. You getting married to the father?"

"I think it's early days for that," she said, a little twinkle glistening in her eyes.

"He's not ready?"

"I don't know, Toph. You tell me."

Topher's gray eyes fixed on her hazel ones.

"So, when Clementine dragged me to you, she packed my bag for me," Pippa said. "I didn't even know where I was going. Of course once I got there and went into my duffel bag, lo and behold, I saw that Clem had thrown in practically a year's supply of condoms. But I had no plans to even need the things, if you'll recall."

Topher nodded. "Yeah, you were so damned stubborn."

"Pot meet kettle," she said. "Anyhow, then you got me drunk and had your wicked way with me—"

"Oh, you take that back right now," he said. "You were completely on board with what happened."

"Ha, on board, indeed. On board the Good Ship

Topher," she said.

"I could think of worse places to be."

She smiled. "As I was saying, you may recall we were both a little preoccupied that night."

"Hot and bothered is a better description," he said, his hands stroking along her knee.

"And in our haste, it seems I completely forgot about precautions, as did you," she said. "Which should kind of be irrelevant because I was on the pill. Except that I was always terrible at remembering to take it every day at the right time. Which is actually sort of a good thing because I hadn't been in a relationship for a superlong time, and it's not like I was sleeping with anyone forever, anyhow."

Topher smiled. "So all those many men from your past you were taunting me with the other day?"

Pippa nodded. "A very distant past. Another lifetime, really. All two of them."

"And you're telling me you're expecting a baby," he said, taking it all in, "with me?"

She held her breath and nodded, squinting her eyes, fearful of his reaction.

"You know when I started to say about how I've had a chance to think about what if it was the last day? And I've given it a lot of consideration since my accident, you know. Well, you've just given me the most perfect scenario for my last day if it were to be that. The only bad thing would be I'd never know my child."

With that he threw his arms around Pippa and kissed her like mad. "I know this sounds crazy since we've really only been on a couple of dates and they weren't even really dates, but being that I've known you my whole life and you were the first female ever to see me naked, not to mention

Love Is in the Heir

the first female I fantasized about nonstop for about five years, how about making an honest man of me and agreeing to marry me, Phillipa Grimaldi?"

Pippa kissed him hard, not wanting to separate from him even to give him an answer. But finally she did, "I'd love nothing more than to spend my life with you," she said. "And him. Or her." She said, pointing to her belly, where he settled his palm, feeling for the life that was growing within her that would bond them as a family forever.

Thank you for reading!

Dear Reader,

I hope you enjoyed **Love is in the Heir**. I've gotta tell you, I honestly had no idea what I was going to write for book four of the **It's Reigning Men** series. I knew I really liked Pippa and wanted to give her her own story, and then after I brought Topher into things in **Bad to the Throne**, I was kind of intrigued about his backstory and why he'd stayed away from his home and family for so long. So I decided whether Pippa liked it or not, she was going to have had a close encounter of the embarrassing kind with Topher from her past, and it would come back to haunt her.

When I started writing the **It's Reigning Men** series, it wasn't necessarily going to be a series. And it had an entirely forgettable title. And a sort of boring, somewhat stiff hero (which my great editor took a whack at, thankfully!). Oh, and I hated the cover: the guy's nose was too long and it just didn't work. That first book (which became **Something in the Heir**) was my take on **Roman Holiday**, a movie I just adore (I mean it's Audrey Hepburn, need I say more?!). I think I called it "Royal Holiday", yawn…which sounded and felt sort of generic. So I was kind of grumpy about it because it just didn't feel "right" yet.

And then it hit me one day out of the blue: **It's Reigning Men**. Of course! How did that take me so long? I love to play with words, so this gave me a great chance to noodle on how many puns I could I come up with involving royalty. Believe me it took some work. My favorite of course was **Bad to the Throne** (not the first time I had a title before I had a clue what my book was going to be—I did the same with my first novel, **Sleeping with Ward Cleaver**). Although my husband may well have trumped me with book five's titles: **Shame of Thrones.** Now *that* I couldn't resist!

What has kept me writing the stories of these interconnected royals from the fictional country of Monaforte is you: letters and emails and Facebook comments and reviews in which you've told me how much you've enjoyed reading these stories. Knowing I have people who are excited to keep delving into this fun world has made it all the more exciting for me each time I start a new book in this series.

I love love love to get feedback from readers, so please, tell me what you liked, what you loved and even what you hated. I'd love to hear from you! You can keep up with the latest news of releases and even get added tidbits and fun extras if you sign up for my newsletter here: http://eepurl.com/baaewn. You can write to me at jenny@jennygardiner.net, and visit me on the web at www.jennygardiner.net. And of course I'm on Facebook (maybe when I should be writing...) https://www.facebook.com/jennygardinerbooks.

And if can ask a huge favor of you, if you are so inclined, I'd love your review of **Love is in the Heir** (and reviews for all of the **It's Reigning Men** series) on Amazon, Goodreads, iBooks, BarnesandNoble.com, etc—I really appreciate your feedback, and it also helps other readers when they're looking for books to read. Reviews are really hard to come by, which is totally understandable because we're all pressed for time and crazy busy. But please know that your review helps authors tremendously and I for one am incredibly grateful for anyone who is able to take the time to review my books and share them with others. You, the reader, have the power to make or break a book! You can find links to all of my books on my Amazon Author page (and even "like" my books there, which Amazon really wants readers to do!) here: http://bit.ly/AmznAuthrPg.

Lastly, many of you have asked for the wedding story, and I want to let you know it will happen. I've been scrambling to keep getting these books out in a timely fashion but I wanted you to know it is on my list to write a detailed depiction of Adrian and Emma's royal wedding just as soon as I can. After all, I've attended their wedding in my mind enough times…it's time to share the grandeur of it all with you!

Thank you again for your ongoing support!

Jenny Gardiner

About Jenny

Jenny Gardiner is the #1 Bestselling Kindle author of the novel ***Slim to None*** and the award-winning novel ***Sleeping with Ward Cleaver***. Her latest works are the ***It's Reigning Men*** series, featuring ***Something in the Heir***, ***Heir Today Gone Tomorrow*** and ***Bad to the Throne, Love is in the Heir***, and the upcoming ***Shame of Thrones***. She also published the memoir ***Winging It: A Memoir of Caring for a Vengeful Parrot Who's Determined to Kill Me***, now re-titled ***Bite Me: a Parrot, a Family and a Whole Lot of Flesh Wounds***; the novels ***Anywhere but Here***, ***Where the Heart Is***; the essay collection ***Naked Man on Main Street***, and ***Accidentally on Purpose*** and ***Compromising Positions*** (writing as Erin Delany); and is a contributor to the humorous dog anthology ***I'm Not the Biggest Bitch in This Relationship***. Her work has been found in Ladies Home Journal, the Washington Post, Marie-Claire.com, and on NPR's Day to Day. She has worked as a professional photographer, an orthodontic assistant as well as a publicist to a United States Senator (where she first learned to write fiction). She's photographed Prince Charles (and her assistant husband got him to chuckle!), Elizabeth Taylor, and the president of Uganda. She and her family now live a less exotic life in Virginia.

Stay tuned for more stories from Monaforte, with book five of the *It's Reigning Men* series, ***Shame of Thrones***, coming December 16, 2015.

Shame of Thrones
By Jenny Gardiner

Read on for a sample of Book five of the **It's Reigning Men** *series:*

SHAME OF THRONES

Chapter One

CLEMENTINE Squires-Thornton knew her mother would absolutely kill her if she found out what her daughter was about to do. And if her mother didn't manage to finish her off, surely her brothers Darcy, or the hot-tempered Eduoardo, certainly would.

But she had no intention of letting an attack of conscience or even a little familial-induced fear stop her now, which she repeatedly told herself in mantra-like fashion as she climbed atop the sticky bar on the legendary party boat the Willy-T, and laid down on her back, wearing only a floral-print string bikini bottom and a broad smile. That she tried to cover her exposed breasts with her long, wavy blonde hair was completely ridiculous. After all, she was clad just about as far opposite of how she'd dress for the Trooping of the Colors or the Queen's birthday or any other royal occasion as she could ever imagine. Modesty at this point was futile.

She'd already far exceeded any sort of usual behavior for her when she'd buckled to a little self-induced peer pressure and ditched that bikini top before she jumped off the upper deck of the steel sailboat into the warm water below, a tradition for revelers at the famed sailboat-cum-bar anchored in the Bight at Norman Island in the British Virgin Islands. But everyone else was doing it, and she figured when in Rome…

Shame of Thrones

Clementine wasn't the type to readily disrobe in public. Probably not one to do so quite willingly in private either, for that matter, unless of course with the right person. As the daughter of a marquess, a nobleman in the small European principality of Monaforte, she was raised to observe strict protocol, and being bare-breasted with a bunch of drunken revelers—strangers, at that—just wasn't part of the program.

As it was, her best friend Pippa Grimaldi would about die if she knew what Clem was up to. But Clementine rationalized that it was partly Pippa's fault she found herself in this predicament. After all, Clem had hastened her good friend off to the Caribbean for a last-minute surprise reunion with Prince Christopher—Topher for short—with whom Pippa had a brief fling at his brother Prince Adrian's wedding. The two had a falling out, and Clementine took it upon herself to fix that, deciding that playing matchmaker was a great way to get her mind off of the recent loss of her beloved father. But once she got Pippa to the tropical paradise, she'd resolved that she was all for playing the Vegas card during this little getaway: what happened in the BVI was simply going to stay in the BVI, and maybe a little less-than-regal behavior was just what she needed to shake up her life a bit.

Which meant she'd be stepping way, way out of her comfort zone because, well, why the hell not? If there was one thing she took away from her father's sudden passing, it was that life was short, and sometimes you just had to throw caution to the wind and live a little.

So it was most convenient when she hit it off with Topher's skipper Sebastian Chevalier, who happened to be his cousin as well. And Sebastian, it seemed—with his wind-tousled light brown hair and sun-kissed highlights that framed a gorgeous tanned face and warm, brown eyes—was just what the therapist ordered. Or at least the therapist would have done so, had he realized how much Sebastian's presence set Clementine's pulse on overload and got her mind off of her woes.

The two readily conspired to ensure that Pippa and Topher would be alone as much as possible, which meant they, too, got plenty of alone-time right from the start. After spending the afternoon snorkeling in the aquamarine Caribbean waters, they'd had great fun fixing a meal for the four of them in the boat's galley kitchen.

Following dinner, Clementine and Sebastian had removed themselves for the evening from the sailboat they were sharing with Pippa and Topher in the hopes of helping to rejuvenate the couple's stalled romance that had fizzled after Adrian's wedding. Which is how Clementine found herself nearly naked atop a bar in a dive bar.

Perhaps the two Painkillers she'd consumed in the past hour or two on top of the wine at dinner had contributed to the diminishing of her standards. But they tasted quite delicious, and fed into her overall warm feeling of being in a lovely place with a lovely man drinking downright lovely drinks. Perhaps they were called Painkillers for a reason. So even though she found herself nearly naked atop a bar, Pippa was hardly even embarrassed. Well, okay, maybe she was squinting shut her cerulean blue eyes, because, yeah, there were a lot of people cheering Sebastian on, and really, she was, after all, pretty exposed. But every now and then she'd open them and look into his eyes and it weirdly instilled a confidence in her.

So when the crowd began cheering for him to peel off

her bikini bottoms, she barely flinched. Hell, she'd seen other women do the same thing earlier in the night, so it's not like she was alone in this behavior. For that matter, there was a line of women waiting for her to finish. It was practically socially acceptable, a veritable cultural norm, right?

The next thing she knew Sebastian was catching the string of one side of her bikini bottoms between his beautiful, straight, white teeth, and ever-so-slowly pulling the strand toward him. And before she knew it, one side of her suit gave way as the crowd whooped and hollered loudly. The other side was a little trickier, and Sebastian had to lean across her taut stomach and with his mouth repeat what he'd done on the other side, which he did with surprising deftness. With great encouragement from the crowd, what happened next was a bit more than Clementine was prepared for, as he used his teeth to edge the front part slightly down to the accompanying roar of approval from the audience that had gathered, though he stopped short of pulling the thing off altogether. Thank goodness for tender mercies.

Her thoughts raced through her mind: first, thank God she'd gotten a fresh waxing before embarking on her Caribbean adventure, but then, holy crap, here she was just about naked in front of a bunch of extremely drunken revelers—were they snapping off pictures and video on their iPhones?—not to mention the extremely handsome and charming Sebastian. But denial kicked in, which kept her from jumping off the bar and fleeing into the water and away from this scene, and instead she closed her eyes and let the Painkiller work its magic, as she repeated in her mind again and again: *what happens in the BVI…*

Jenny Gardiner

Before she knew it, the bartender had poured a shot of local favorite Pusser's rum into her navel, and Sebastian, who she'd known for roughly, oh, maybe a half a day at that point, proceeded to slurp the liquor off of her body as if they'd been intimate for ages. Which, bizarrely, felt absolutely perfect to Clementine.

It was a good thing her family was never going to learn about this.

Chapter Two

SEBASTIAN could not believe his good fortune. He was thrilled enough when Clementine had boarded their sailboat earlier in the day. He knew the woman was bringing Topher's fling down to the BVI to try to buoy up the couple's nascent romance, but he hadn't expected her to be so beguiling. Athletic and gorgeous with long, lean legs and a beautifully-proportioned body, she was far more than he could have hoped for as a guest on his forty-foot catamaran. At the time, he could barely contain images that kept popping into his mind of her down on her knees, taking him into her mouth, peering up at him with those blue, blue eyes, that long blond ponytail bobbing as she worked—he was a guy, after all. But he knew there wasn't much chance of that. After all, he'd never even met the woman before. Plus she was here on business of sorts.

Yet fast-forward a few short hours and first she shocks him by following protocol on the party boat the Willy-T and removing her bikini top before jumping into the water below, and now she was spread out before him on top of the Willy-T bar, and he'd managed to peel off most of what remained of her bathing suit in a pretty erotic little scene, despite the crowd of cheering partiers surrounding the two of them. It took all the restraint he could muster to not remove the thing altogether. Nevertheless, here he was now, using his tongue to lick a shot of rum from her belly button. If he'd have been in Vegas, this would be the equivalent of three dollar signs in a row on a slot machine.

Jenny Gardiner

Jackpot, indeed.

As he leaned over to suck the liquid off of her body, he glanced up, his eyes making contact with hers just past those spectacular breasts he'd tried not to overtly ogle since she'd removed her top before taking the plunge. He'd spent many a night at the Willy-T, but never had he had the great pleasure of accompanying the most beautiful woman on board, let alone be the one to partake in extremely sexy body shots with.

Sebastian couldn't exactly hide his pleasure, what with him still wearing his swimming trunks from earlier that had tented up on the front. At least he was facing the bar, so a little less obvious. Plus he was grateful they were somewhat loose, as opposed to the usual European-style "root suit" swimwear, which he opted not to use while in the Caribbean.

As he finished the long, slow sensual lapping of the first shot, he fought all of his brain's urging to just keep moving that tongue to even more interesting spots on her body. But then the bartender did the damnedest thing: he drizzled rum across Clementine's breasts and the gauntlet was thrown.

Sebastian looked at her rack, then looked into her eyes, and she gave a small nod, which he took as permission enough. He leaned forward and first licked the rum that had trickled down toward the base of her neck, beginning a trail along her cleavage. The crowd went nuts in the background, but he managed to tune them out quite readily as his tongue worked its way across first one nipple, then the other, lapping and circling and making sure he got up every last drop of liquid. After all, he didn't want to leave behind a sticky mess. As much as he wanted to settle his mouth over one of those things and just spend some time sucking, he thought that would be going a little overboard considering they'd just met that afternoon, so he opted out.

He glanced up at Clementine who smiled as if she was actually enjoying herself, which made him grin back at her with a sly wink.

Of course the bartender wouldn't stop there. In between pours he and his fellow bartenders were refilling drinks in record time, with a crowd that wanted more, more, more. And he clearly planned to give it to them, because before Sebastian could blink, the bottle of rum was hovering just above her pelvis. Sebastian gulped. Now *this* was nothing he'd ever expected to be doing in front of a crowd.

He leaned over and whispered into Clementine's ear.

"I'm okay if you're ready to call it a night."

Clem turned her head to him.

"Kiss me," she said so that only he could hear her.

Sebastian wasted no time pressing his lips to hers as his tongue reached out, searching for hers. As much as he wanted his hands to explore all of those exposed parts of her, he didn't want to grope her in front of all of those people. Which was a little weird considering he'd already licked around the better half her body, so go figure. Instead he threaded his fingers through her hair, massaging her scalp with his nails as their mouths met.

When they both came up for air, Clementine whispered to him.

"You swear to God no one will ever know about this?"

Sebastian shrugged.

"Neither of us knows anyone in this place, right? I

can't imagine how it would get out. These people are all visitors on holiday: just ships passing in the night, never to be seen again. Besides, people do this all the time here. It's not as if it's something outrageous or unusual."

The two laughed at that one. Sebastian knew that this was so beyond scandalous for someone like Clementine, it was almost socially acceptable. She'd been repeating aloud all evening that life was short, and sometimes it was okay to just do stupid things.

They both looked at the bartender and finally Clementine gave another barely discernable nod, and he began to pour.

Shame of Thrones
coming December 16, 2015.

Made in the USA
Monee, IL
09 October 2020